THE
IMPOSSIBLE
QUEST

TO BECK & RADHIAH, FOR ALL THEIR HARD WORK
MAKING THE IMPOSSIBLE QUEST THE VERY BEST
IT CAN BE—THANK YOU!

First American Edition 2016
Kane Miller, A Division of EDC Publishing

Text copyright © Kate Forsyth 2015

First published by Scholastic Press, a division of Scholastic Australia Pty Limited in 2015.
Cover illustration and maps on pages iv-vi by Jeremy Reston.
Dove brooch on page 14 by Radhiah Chowdhury, copyright © Scholastic Australia, 2015.
Map on page 57 by Keisha Galbraith, copyright © Scholastic Australia, 2015.
Logo design by blacksheep-uk.com.
This edition published under license from Scholastic Australia Pty Limited.
Internal photography: brick texture on page i © GiorgioMagini|istockphoto.com;
castle on page ii and folios © ivan-96|istockphoto.com; shield on page 48 ©
nwinter|istockphoto.com; dove on page 48 © grmarc|istockphoto.com.au; clouds
on page 48 © comzeal|istockphoto.com; gem on page 48 © MariaTkach|istockphoto.
com; map, compass and texture on page 53 © nicoolay|istockphoto.com; reverse
skull on page 139 © Frankie_Lee|istockphoto.com; crowned heart on page 170 ©
CelloFun|istockphoto.com;parchment on page 176 © zoomstudio|istockphoto.com;
parchment on pages 177-178 © 4khz|istockphoto.com; parchment on page 179 ©
hidesy|istockphoto.com; parchment on page 181 © iSailorr|istockphoto.com.

For information contact:
Kane Miller, A Division of EDC Publishing
P.O. Box 470663
Tulsa, OK 74147-0663
www.kanemiller.com
www.edcpub.com
www.usbornebooksandmore.com

Library of Congress Control Number: 2015945041

Printed and bound in the United States of America
6 7 8 9 10

ISBN: 978-1-61067-417-1

KATE FORSYTH

THE IMPOSSIBLE QUEST

THE DROWNED KINGDOM

Kane Miller
A DIVISION OF EDC PUBLISHING

Map of Wolfhaven & Surrounding Lands

The Witchwood

Crowthorne Castle

Rosemorran River

Blackmoor Bog

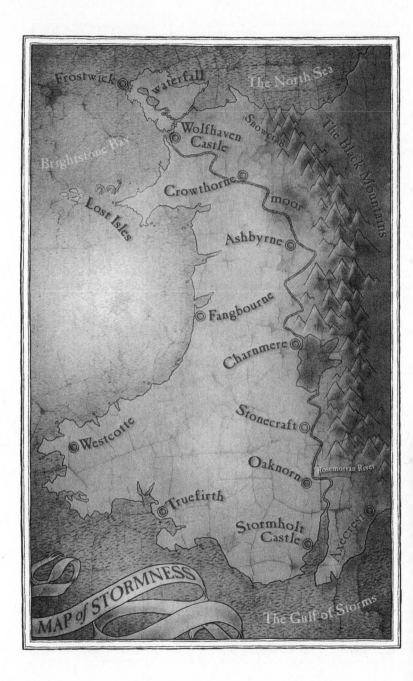

FIRE SPELL

If I can raise the bones of long-dead dragons, I can do anything. There is no need to be afraid . . .

Quinn gazed into the campfire, her hands clenched hard upon her rowan witch's staff. The flames guttered in the sea wind, eerie shadows skulking across the faces of her friends.

Elanor sat with her chin on her knees, her arms wrapped around her legs, her forehead knotted with worry. Her back rested along the dark curve of Quickthorn's body. The unicorn had run far that day and was glad to lie by the fire, his head resting on his forelegs, black spiraling horn gleaming faintly in the firelight.

Sebastian stroked the glossy scales of the baby dragon that lay sleeping in his lap, her scales reflecting gold in the flames. Beside him sat Jack Spry, amusing herself by juggling pinecones. Until recently, Quinn and her friends had thought Jack was a boy, but she had just admitted that it had been a disguise all along. It was hard to believe. She looked every inch a ragamuffin boy in her tattered breeches and jerkin and her short, tousled curls.

Tom, meanwhile, sat stirring a pot of soup that he had made from water, seaweed and some cockles they had scraped from the rocks. Above their heads, the griffin Rex was crouched in the branches of a windblown black pine, tearing at his dinner with his strong, curved beak.

"I wish Rex would catch us something to eat, too," Sebastian said morosely.

"He caught seabirds for Fergus and Wulfric, as well as for your little dragon," Tom said. "He deserves to eat his dinner in peace."

"He could spare us a leg or two, surely," said Sebastian.

"Do you want to try and get one from him?" Tom asked with a grin.

Sebastian eyed the griffin's fierce beak and strong talons and shook his head with a reluctant laugh.

Fergus and Wulfric had both lifted their heads and wagged their tails at the sound of their names, but now lay back down and went to sleep. The sight of them gave Quinn hope. The Grand Teller's prophecy had said:

WHEN THE WOLF LIES DOWN WITH THE WOLFHOUND,
AND THE STONES OF THE CASTLE SING,
THE SLEEPING HEROES SHALL WAKE FOR THE CROWN,
AND THE BELLS OF VICTORY RING.

GRIFFIN FEATHER AND UNICORN'S HORN,
SEA SERPENT SCALE AND DRAGON'S TOOTH,
BRING THEM TOGETHER AT FIRST LIGHT OF DAWN,
AND YOU SHALL SEE THIS SPELL'S TRUTH.

The first line of the prophecy had come true, with the wolf and the wolfhound now friends instead of enemies. The second half was almost complete. Quinn and her friends had managed to find a unicorn, a griffin and—only a few hours earlier—a dragon. Now they had to find a sea serpent scale and then, somehow, get back into Wolfhaven Castle without being caught.

A shiver ran over her. Quinn had seen such evil these past few weeks. She had seen bloody battles, cruel treachery and black magic. She, Tom and Sebastian were only thirteen years old. Elanor was younger still, not yet thirteen. How could they possibly hope to stand against Lord Mortlake and his wicked wife?

She shivered again. They had barely escaped with their lives that day. They were all hungry, cold, exhausted and dressed in little more than rags. They had no boat, no map and no idea where to find a sea serpent.

Never had their quest seemed so impossible.

Tom ladled out the watery soup and the group sipped from their bowls.

"At least it's hot," Elanor said.

Sebastian had gulped his soup down in a single

slurp and now stared into the empty bowl morosely. "Any more?"

Tom shook his head.

Quinn braced herself for the two boys to start arguing again. To her surprise, there was silence. It was only then that she realized how much they had all changed since their quest began. Tom and Sebastian were no longer just allies—they were friends. Elanor was no longer the timid girl who lived up in her tower. Quinn looked over to where her friend was running her fingers through Quickthorn's mane.

And I? Quinn looked at her witch's staff. Just weeks ago, she would never have dreamed that she would have gained her witch powers so soon.

Sebastian was still staring at his empty bowl. "I think I miss your mam's cooking more than anything else," he told Tom. "Well, aside from my bed."

"I just miss Mam," said Tom. "Hey, Quinn, could you try that spell Wilda used in the Witchwood to show us what's happening?"

Quinn was taken aback. "I don't know. I've never done it before."

"But you remember the words, don't you? You always remember stuff like that."

Quinn wrapped her arms around her knees. "I don't know . . . I don't think we should. It feels wrong. It feels . . . dangerous."

"It can't be more dangerous than battling giant bog-men," Sebastian said. "Or fighting off the Beast of Blackmoor Bog. You're a witch now, Quinn. You have powers we never imagined were possible."

"Don't you want to see what's happened to our families?" Tom reasoned. "Surely you can conjure a vision of them for all of us."

Quinn remembered the vision she and the others had seen in Wilda's obsidian ball. The people of Wolfhaven Castle had been crammed together in the castle dungeon, with nothing to sleep on but damp straw. All had been bruised and battered. Lord Wolfgang, Elanor's father, had been so weak he could hardly stand. Mistress Pippin, Tom's mother, had had a black eye, while Arwen, Quinn's mistress and teacher, had looked as pale and fragile as a paper doll.

It had been awful to see them that way.

"I'm not a witch yet," Quinn answered. "I'm still only an apprentice."

Tom grinned. "Really? That's the first time I've heard you admit that! Come on, Quinn, you've won your staff now. What more do you need? Doesn't that make you a witch?"

She hunched her shoulders.

"Are you scared?" Jack jeered.

"Of course not!" Quinn snapped. "I don't have an obsidian ball."

"But Arwen doesn't use an obsidian ball when she scries for visions," Elanor said. "She just looks into the fire. I've seen her do it."

"Maybe she doesn't know *how* to do it," Jack said.

Quinn flashed Jack a look of disdain. "Of course I do. It's just that an obsidian ball makes it much easier for you non-witches to see."

Jack tossed up a wheel of spinning pinecones. "Well, I don't need to see anything, anyway, so don't you worry about me."

"Can't we just try, Quinn? Please?" Elanor pleaded. "I need to see my father."

Quinn ducked her head down. "I should have eyebright water, and angelica and hawthorn leaves to burn—"

"You're always picking bunches of weeds and flowers and sticking them in your pack," Tom said. "I'm sure you have something that will work."

Quinn thought of the mugwort she had picked from a ditch a few days ago. It was a useful plant for travelers. A poultice made of the crushed leaves helped relieve aches, pains, blisters and bruises, all of which the children suffered in plenty. As Wilda had shown them, though, it had other uses . . .

Tom saw her expression change. "I knew it! What do you have?"

"Mugwort," she replied reluctantly. "If you breathe its smoke, it brings visions and prophecies. But it's poisonous. We've already breathed it in once, when Wilda did the scrying spell for us in the Witchwood. Remember the nightmares we all had?"

"After everything we've seen, I can handle a few nightmares," Tom said. "I have to know if my mam's all right."

"Surely just a little will do the trick?" Elanor asked hesitantly. "I'm so worried about my father. I can't bear to think of him so sick and weak. Please, let's find out what's happening to them all."

"I'd like to see if any of our messages got through to my father," Sebastian said. "I'm hoping to see him riding at the head of an army, his sword held high."

"I thought Wilda told you that she had just pretended to send our messages out," Quinn said.

"One might have made it through," Sebastian said. "You never know."

Quinn hesitated. She felt such a strong sense of disquiet, as if eyes were watching them from the darkness. Yet all the beasts were quiet and peaceful and Fergus had not stirred. If strangers prowled nearby, the wolfhound would have alerted them all by now.

"Don't you want to see how Arwen is?" Tom asked.

Tears stung Quinn's eyes. Arwen had raised her ever since Quinn had been found on Wolfhaven's shores in a wicker basket as a baby, abandoned with no clues to her identity. She loved Arwen as if the Grand Teller truly was her mother.

"Of course I want to see her," she replied huskily. "But I'm so afraid that it's—" Her voice failed her.

"Too late?" Elanor finished.

Quinn nodded.

They sat in silence. Sparks flew up like fireflies towards the dark sky.

"So Quinn isn't worried she'll fail?" Tom's voice was wondering, not mocking, but heat rushed to Quinn's cheeks anyway. She looked away, biting her lip.

"You've won your witch's staff," Elanor said.

"And you made that bog flower grow until it was big enough to eat the Beast!" Sebastian added with a grim smile.

"Don't forget the flying dragon bones!" said Tom.

They all looked over to where the dragon bones lay scattered over the rock, gleaming faintly in the moonlight. Somehow, Quinn had brought the skeleton of a long-dead dragon to life. She and Sebastian and Jack had flown high and far and swift on its back, till the sun had set and the magic had come to an end. The dragon had fallen back into a scatter of old bones, right on the edge of the cliff.

All her life, Quinn had longed for strong magical powers. She had imagined winning her witch's staff and bag of tell-stones, stalking through the castle with her white robes swishing and everyone gazing at her in amazement, whispering: "They say she is the most powerful witch in the country!" She had pictured the look of pride on Arwen's face and Lord Wolfgang's gruff words of commendation. Surely then the people of Wolfhaven would be glad they'd taken her in and offered her a home when she had none. Surely then they'd proudly claim her as one of their own.

Quinn had her staff now and a bag of tell-stones hung from her belt beside her obsidian witch's knife. She wore the talisman of the Oak King, an old wooden face that whispered wisdom into her mind. She and her friends had battled a two-headed giant and outwitted a black-hearted witch.

And yet, she'd never been more afraid.

Quinn drew in a deep breath, squared her shoulders, dug out the bundle of mugwort and threw the herb on the fire. Smoke billowed up at once, eye-watering and pungent. Fergus snorted and got up, sending the little wolf cub tumbling. He moved away from the fire with a reproachful backward glance and Wulfric trotted after him. They settled down again under the pine tree, well away from the smoke.

Everyone was coughing. Quinn shielded her eyes with her hand and croaked the words of the spell:

> "BLAZING FIRE SHINING BRIGHT,
> GIVE US NOW THE SECOND SIGHT,
> PART THE VEILS OF THE NIGHT,
> SHOW US OUR KIN IN YOUR LIGHT."

Then, her pulse beating uncomfortably fast, Quinn stared into the fire.

SEA RISE UP,
SKY FALL DOWN

Quinn saw a ship tossing on a wild, stormy sea, its sails torn to rags by the wind. Dark figures labored desperately to bring the ship under control, but waves crashed over the bow and foamed across the decks. The crew scrambled to stop themselves from being swept overboard.

A round window in the stern was lit up. Quinn could see into the grandly furnished cabin within. A tall man in a green velvet doublet was comforting a white-faced woman who held a crying baby in her arms. The baby was wrapped in a waterfall of silk and lace. As the ship plunged down a wave, the woman was flung to the ground. The man hurried to help her up, taking the baby from her and tucking it firmly in a beautifully carved oak cradle. He turned back to the woman, who'd begun to weep. The man kissed her and held her close. He had a thin, proud face, with curly black hair and a pointed beard. His eyes were a striking turquoise green in his swarthy face. An intricately carved brooch fastened his fur-trimmed cloak around his shoulders. It was shaped like a dove carrying a heart-shaped ruby in its beak.

The wind howled. Quinn thought she could hear the chanting of words.

"SEA RISE UP, SKY FALL DOWN,
SEA SWALLOW, SKY DROWN."

The sea heaved up in black walls of water, the wave crests breaking white like shards of glass. Spray flew. Rain pelted.

The ship was flung upon rocks with a groan of cracking timber. Water crashed through the cabin, knocking down the lantern, sweeping the man and woman apart. The sea tore at the broken ship with white teeth and claws, then gulped it down into its black, gaping maw.

Quinn was slowly but savagely sucked into the scene. All the world spun, a tornado of white, streaming water. She saw the ship's ragged masts and ropes slanting against a lightning-silver sky. A gleeful laugh echoed on the wind.

The sea was slithering . . . it was full of serpents, writhing, twisting, thrashing around. Their huge silver bodies filled the water. One reared high, fanged mouth agape. Quinn cried out.

Another voice chanted:

"Willow, call to oak, Hear the spell I spoke.
Oak, come to willow, Ride safe on wave's billow."

The waves drew her away from the serpent and safely to shore. A willow's green fronds hung down over her. Quinn felt herself lifted free of the water. An old man wound her all around with supple willow stems till she was wrapped in leafy green.

"Safe and sound, by willow bound,
Never to be found, by willow crowned."

The shore disappeared. The vision changed.

Now Quinn was crouched somewhere. Stone below her, cold darkness all around. She could not even see her hands. She felt around frantically, eyes searching the gloom, then at last looked up.

Far above, perched on the cliff face, loomed a tower with one window alight. A woman stood there, her face cast into shadow. She held up one hand and a ring on her finger blazed red. Storm clouds roiled. Thunder growled and lightning flashed. Then a thin ray of red light shot out from the woman's ring. It pierced the maelstrom, moving from side to side, as if searching. The woman was an enemy, Quinn was sure of it. Quinn shrank back, but the light found and pinned her. "I see you," cried a voice. "I know you."

The voice sounded familiar, but Quinn had neither time nor breath to wonder why. The red-hot ray of light was skewering her to the ground. It widened and became a spear of fire. With all her strength, Quinn rolled away. She scrambled up the cliff face, blundering through the darkness as the red ray swept from side to side, searching for her.

Quinn was so cold, her muscles cramped. Rain and spray lashed her face. She slipped and slid backward. At last, she managed to crawl over the lip of the cliff. Lightning flashed and Quinn saw a woman peering down into a well of dark water. She wore a long slinky dress that glittered strangely. Black hair coiled down her back. "I see you," she hissed. "I know you."

Quinn saw with horror that the woman had only

one eye. Then serpents writhed up from the well. Quinn cowered as they swarmed towards her, growing and growing till they towered above her, fangs bared.

She screamed.

"Quinn, wake up!"

Hands seized her, shook her. Quinn struck out blindly and heard a cry of pain. She struck out again and again, punching, kicking.

"Quinn, stop it! Wake up! Wake up!"

Slowly she became aware of light against her eyelids and the sound of weeping. She shook back her hair and sat up. Her heart was thumping. Her friends were crouched around her in the firelit darkness.

"It's all right, Quinn," Elanor soothed. "We're here. Everything is all right."

Sebastian held one hand to his cheek, which bore an angry red mark. "And you've got one mean punch."

"I . . . I'm sorry . . . I was having the worst vision. I felt like I was cast into it."

"What did you see?" Elanor clutched her hand. Her face was wet with tears. "Did you see them, too? They all looked so sick and weak! My father could scarcely raise his head." She choked back another sob.

Quinn stared at her in confusion.

"My mam was doing her best," Tom said, his face drawn, "but she's so thin now. They can't be giving the prisoners much food." His voice broke.

Quinn remembered the spell. "I . . . I didn't see Arwen . . . or the others."

Sebastian looked surly. "Me either," he said. "I saw my sisters in new dresses, dancing and laughing. My parents were feasting. They're all celebrating the Harvest Festival. They have no idea that I'm running for my life, or that I almost got sucked into the bog!"

Quinn saw that Jack was hanging back, arms crossed over her chest, her eyes reddened and inflamed. Tears ran down her grubby cheeks.

"What did you see?" Quinn asked gently.

Jack's face contorted. "Do you think I wanted to see *my* family? They're dead! All of them. And I had to watch them die again!" She jumped up, dashing the tears from her face. "I can't bear it. I have to go."

"I'm sorry." Tears welled up in Quinn's eyes. "I did warn you—"

"I thought we were looking to see *your* families, not mine! I wanted to see how Mistress Pippin was, too. She was kind to me. If I'd known I'd see my whole family being murdered again . . ." Jack snatched up her battered jacket.

"Please don't go," Quinn said. "I'm sorry, I didn't know what visions the mugwort smoke would bring. Please don't go rushing off into the darkness."

"It's not safe," Tom said. "You could go over the edge of the cliff."

Jack stood undecided for a moment, then threw down her jacket. "I'll go at first light."

Elanor turned to Quinn. "What did you see?" she asked timidly. "It must have been bad. You were screaming and thrashing around."

Quinn looked away. The vision was already dissolving. "There was a storm . . . and a shipwreck . . . and snakes," she murmured.

The others looked at each other.

"Let's hope your vision is not prophetic," Sebastian said grimly.

HERE BE SEA SERPENTS

Elanor stood on the crest of the cliff, staring across mist-wreathed forest and hills. The sea wind blew her ragged skirts around her legs and she had to hold back her hair to stop it whipping her face.

To the north, a castle seemed to float high in the air, its towers and gatehouses rising from the heavy white fog. Elanor knew every tower and staircase. It was Wolfhaven Castle, where she had lived since birth. She knew it was sturdy and strong, built of stone on a high rocky crag. But right now, it looked as though it might simply drift away in the wind.

Elanor heard a footstep behind her and turned. Quinn had wrapped her shawl close against the cold dawn. She gazed at the castle, her sea-green eyes looking too big for her pale, narrow face.

"Don't you wish we could just go home and find all our friends and family there to welcome us?" Elanor said into the chilly morning.

Quinn nodded and slipped one arm through her friend's. "I don't think we'd get much of a welcome if we went there now."

Elanor blinked back tears, remembering the castle the way they had last seen it—hazed in smoke, black-armored knights seizing all the castle folk. Lord Mortlake had been standing on the ramparts, his tusked helmet silhouetted against the dawn, bog-men scuttling out at his command.

"We'll find that sea serpent scale and make Lord Mortlake sorry he ever invaded!" Elanor cried.

Quinn squeezed her hand.

Tom came along the cliff top towards them, Fergus and Wulfric trotting at his heels, as always. "I found some eggs for breakfast." He opened his hand to reveal a clutch of brown speckled bird's eggs. "Let's eat and make some plans."

The girls followed him down the slope to where the campfire glowed in the shelter of the bent pine tree. Quickthorn stood cropping the grass beneath it, his hooves and horn as black as the witch's blade at Quinn's waist. He lifted his head and whickered, and Elanor went over to stroke his satiny neck.

Tom rummaged in his pack for his frying pan. Sebastian and Jack came out of the forest, their arms full of kindling. The baby dragon gamboled along beside them. Every now and then, she spluttered out a spray of fiery sparks and Sebastian had to hurry to stamp them out. "It's lucky it's so damp and misty, else we'd have a wildfire on our hands," he said. "Can you teach a baby dragon not to spit sparks?"

"Train her like you'd train a puppy," Tom advised, breaking the eggs into the pan and whisking them with a fork.

"Splash water at her every time she does it," Jack suggested. "Keep a bucketful handy."

"She might fly away and not come back if you do that," Quinn said. "Then what would we do?"

Jack shrugged. "Pull out a tooth before you do

it, then. That's all you need, isn't it, for that spell of yours? A dragon tooth?"

"I don't know . . ." Quinn was grave faced and thoughtful. "The beasts have helped us so much on our quest. I think we need *them*, too, and not just what they can give us."

"Besides, I don't want to hurt her." Sebastian dropped the kindling by the fire, then gave the baby dragon a rub between her pointed ears.

"And I thought you were tough," Jack teased.

Sebastian grinned over his shoulder at Jack. "What I'd like to do is train her to spit out sparks when I need her to," he said. "She could have been helpful this morning when I was trying to relight the fire, but all she wanted to do then was chase butterflies."

He built up the fire deftly, then sat beside it, scooping up the baby dragon and cradling her against the soft velvet of his jacket. The dragon, worn out, closed her eyes and fell asleep. Sebastian couldn't help but smile.

"She needs a name," Elanor said. "What shall we call her?"

"I'm going to name her Beltaine," Sebastian said firmly. "It has two meanings, see? It means bright fire and it's also the Fire Festival when she was born. It's perfect for her."

Elanor gazed at Sebastian, taken aback. The name *was* perfect, but she was surprised the hot-tempered squire had come up with it. Perhaps there was more to Sebastian than she had realized.

"So what do you all plan to do now?" Jack asked.

"If we're to go and hunt down a sea serpent, we'll need a boat," Quinn answered.

"That's going to be hard," Sebastian declared.

"We'll have to steal one," Tom reasoned.

"It won't be stealing," Elanor said. "That's my father's castle and the boats are his. We're simply borrowing one."

"All right. We *borrow* a boat, then." Tom grinned at her.

"We need to find one big enough for all of us," Elanor said, looking at their menagerie of beasts.

"Yes," said Tom. "And then we just need to figure out how to find a sea serpent."

"But how?" Elanor asked.

"We'll need some kind of map or chart," Tom said.

"One that says 'here be sea serpents'?" Quinn laughed. "With a nice little picture to show us exactly where they are."

"Maybe the boat we steal—I mean, borrow—will have a sea chart in it," Elanor said. "You never know, it may have the home of the sea serpents marked on it or something."

"You could ask around in town," Jack said. "Someone will know where to find a sea serpent."

"We don't know what's happened in the town," Elanor said. "When we fled Wolfhaven, the townsfolk did not even know the castle had been invaded! Lord Mortlake attacked in darkness and secrecy . . ."

"Under the cover of that strange, thick mist," Quinn added.

"The townsfolk were just going about their everyday business. They didn't even know that we'd spent all night fighting off invaders." Tom shook his head in amazement.

Jack stared at them incredulously. "And you didn't

think to tell them?!" she exclaimed.

Sebastian's cheeks reddened. "We didn't have a choice," he explained. "How could they have done anything? The castle guard were already taken. The last thing we wanted was a group of bakers and chandlers coming up against Lord Mortlake's army. They wouldn't have lasted a second . . ."

"And we just don't know what's been happening since. Perhaps the townsfolk have all been taken prisoner too." Elanor's brow puckered with anxiety at the thought.

"Surely not! The dungeons are not big enough to hold so many people," Sebastian said. "He probably has them all cowed into submission. But surely they'll help us when they realize that we're out of the castle and trying to free everyone."

Jack nodded grudgingly. "I didn't see anyone worrying about the castle when I went through the town, either," she admitted. "I mean, I wasn't really paying attention—"

"You were too busy carting off the castle silverware!" Sebastian interrupted. Jack blushed.

"Good thing I did, or I wouldn't have been around in Crowthorne to save your backside!" she fired back. "Anyway, it didn't look like anyone even had a clue what had happened in the castle. And that fog was still everywhere."

Quinn frowned in the direction of the castle, still wreathed in thick mist. "It's still there now. I wonder why?" she mused aloud.

"Well, the mist sticking around works in our favor," Tom said, "if our plan is to sneak in, steal a boat and sail away before anyone knows we've been there. We have to be very careful. We can't afford to get caught again."

"What about the beasts?" Sebastian asked, cuddling the sleeping dragon closer. "We can't risk taking them near other people."

"No," Tom agreed. "What if just Quinn and I go? We could scout around, see what we can find out."

"But it's my castle," Elanor said. "I want to see what has happened to it."

"That's why you can't go," Tom said. "You're the lady of the castle, everyone knows your face."

"He's right," Sebastian said. "Besides, we need to keep you safe, just in case something has happened to your father. You're his heir."

Elanor looked sick at the thought.

"But I don't see why I have to stay," Sebastian said. "I'm the biggest and the strongest. I'm the only one trained to fight. I should be the one going."

"That's why you're the best person to guard Ela," Tom said. "Besides, it's not strength we need right now. We're not going to fight. That'd be stupid. We'd have no chance against Lord Mortlake's army. No, we're going to sneak around and spy, not fight."

"I see," Sebastian said, but he did not look happy. He hated to be left out of anything.

"Besides, I don't think your Beltaine would like you to leave her just yet," Elanor went on, waving at the little dragon curled so peacefully in Sebastian's lap.

That thought cheered Sebastian up. "That's true."

"Well, I'm in no hurry to get back to Wolfhaven," Jack declared. "I've had enough of those bog-men to last me *two* lifetimes. Do you still want me to get a message to Ashbyrne?"

"If you're headed away from Wolfhaven, then yes," said Sebastian. "But you'll have to remember what I say, as we haven't any paper."

Jack smiled and tapped her temple. "I remember everything. Trick of my trade."

"All right, this is where you go and this is what you have to say." Sebastian drew a rough map in the ashes. Jack listened intently as he told her what she should say to his father, then jumped up.

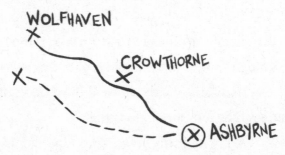

"Right, then. I'll be on my way," she said. "It'll take me some time to get through the Crowthorne bogs and moors, but I'll go as fast as I can. Fun as it's been, I'm looking forward to a bed and a real meal."

She tipped her hat at them, then went on her way, whistling. Within minutes, she was out of sight in the forest, heading due south. The four friends were left sitting around the fire in the silent morning.

"So how on earth are we going to find out where to look for a sea serpent?" Elanor said at last.

"I could ask Sylvan." Quinn lifted up the medallion of the Oak King which hung around her neck on a leather thong. She looked down into the wise old face carved from bog oak, his hair and beard formed in curling leafy fronds. "Sylvan," she whispered. "Can you tell me where the sea serpents live?"

The carved wooden eyes opened and looked up into Quinn's. Elanor found the Oak King utterly magical and wondrous, and sometimes wished that Arwen had gifted him to her. But then she looked down at the moonstone ring glowing silvery blue on her finger and changed her mind. She loved her moonstone ring, which had saved her life several times already.

Quinn sat still, staring into the face of the Oak King as his lips slowly moved. Elanor thought she could hear a faint echo of what he said.

"Most answers can be found in stories," she repeated aloud.

"You heard him?"

Elanor nodded. "Very faintly. Like a very old, very tired voice."

I am very old and very tired, Sylvan said, and shut his wooden eyes.

"What does he mean?" Tom wondered.

"I don't know . . ." Quinn looked away into the distance. "I heard a story about sea serpents once, when I was a little girl. I used to go down to listen to the tales of an old sailor who lived in the fishing village at the foot of the cliffs. He was the one who found me when I was a baby. He said he'd sailed all around the world and seen all sorts of marvelous things . . ."

"Maybe we could go to the fishing village and talk to him now." Tom jumped to his feet.

"And maybe he could help us find a boat?" Elanor suggested.

"Maybe." Quinn stood with new hope, her hand grasped firmly around her witch's staff. She hoped the old sailor would still be where she last saw him. "It's worth a try."

4

THE CASTLE
IN THE MIST

The wild griffin crouched on a rock, staring at the four friends with fierce yellow eyes, his tufted tail swaying from side to side.

"I need you to take Quinn on your back, too," Tom pleaded. "Please, Rex. It's not for long."

The griffin hissed through his beak.

"Please?"

The griffin rose to his haunches, his claws extended, his beak gnashing.

With a sigh, Tom got out his flute and began to play every soothing song he knew. The music calmed the great magical beast and soon his tail stopped lashing and his claws retracted back into his lion paws.

"We're going to climb on your back now," Tom warned the beast. "Both me and Quinn."

The griffin slitted his eyes.

"I'd hold on tight," Tom advised Quinn, who did her best to pretend she was not frightened. He swung up onto the beast's back and held his hand out to her.

As Quinn approached the griffin, he hissed through his beak. She jumped back.

"Shh, Rex," Tom said, stroking the golden feathers. "Please, we need you."

The griffin glared at Quinn but stopped hissing. She hesitantly climbed onto the beast's back, holding tight to Tom's waist.

Fergus whined and gazed at Tom with beseeching brown eyes. The wolfhound hated it when Tom flew into the sky on the griffin's back, leaving him behind. "Stay, Fergus," Tom said sternly. "I won't be long."

Fergus's ears sank. Wulfric whimpered.

"Be careful," Elanor said. "Please don't get caught."

"We'll come and rescue you if you are," Sebastian assured them.

Tom urged Rex into the air.

Higher and higher they climbed, till the camp was left far behind them. The sea stretched out to the cloud-massed horizon on their left, like crumpled gray cloth. To their right, mist-hung meadows rolled into forest. The gray bulk of the castle crouched on its rock far above, only its towers visible above the haze. It was still early, the sun just peeping above the mountains.

Quinn clung to him so tightly that Tom could scarcely breathe, but he said nothing. He knew it was terrifying being so high. His heart still pounded hard, even after a week of flying on the griffin's back.

In little more than twenty minutes, the castle was close enough for Tom to guide the griffin to the ground. Quinn clambered down on shaky legs and Tom patted Rex's neck and told him to go back to the others. "I'll call you if I need you," he said.

The griffin bowed his head then launched back into the sky. A few strong beats of his wings and the beast was almost out of sight, high in the sky.

Tom and Quinn made their way into the woods, heading towards the castle. Before long, they too were enveloped in mist. It flowed clammily all around them in an impenetrable, gray curtain. Tangled twigs sprang at them from the murk, whipping at their faces, tearing their clothes, tangling their feet.

"This mist is all wrong," Quinn said. "It feels wrong. It smells wrong. I don't like it."

"I don't like it either," Tom said, "but at least it means no one can see us."

They crept onward, keeping close together, eyes fixed on their feet. Brambles snaked around their ankles. There was no path. Tom could only find his way by peering at the compass he held in his hand. Finally, they reached the foot of the castle rock. Cliffs reared steeply before them, as slippery and black as a wall made of obsidian.

"The fishing village is right at the foot of the cliffs," Quinn whispered. "If we head towards the sea, we should find the steps that lead down to the village from the castle."

"Can you find the way in all this mist?" Tom asked.

"I think so. Listen, I can hear waves. We must be near the sea."

On they stumbled, keeping the cliffs on their right.

The booming sound of waves came closer, muffled by the mist. The woods were ghostly quiet. No birds twittered, no squirrels scampered. There was no sign of anyone out gathering mushrooms or searching for kindling. It was eerie.

At last, Tom came to a set of steps cut deep into the rock. To his right, they climbed straight up a narrow cleft in the rock to the castle above. To his left, they led down to a narrow shingle beach. The mist was thinner there, stirred by the sea breeze. Tom could see tiny stone cottages clustered together on the shore and small boats pulled up on the shingle. He made out the figures of men, sitting on rocks, mending nets, while women, their skirts kilted above their knees, gathered seaweed from the shore. Everyone moved slowly, as if they were exhausted. The mist hung on their bodies like damp cloth.

"It's so strange," Quinn whispered. "It's like the castle was never attacked. It looks just like any ordinary day . . . except for the mist."

"Perhaps Sebastian is right, and Lord Mortlake has them all frightened into submission. Perhaps there are soldiers on guard, making sure they don't escape or fight back." Tom scanned the scene, but it was hard to see much with the mist blanketing everything. "Do you know where to find this old sailor who has traveled the world?"

"He lives in one of those fishing huts, but I don't remember which one," Quinn whispered. "What shall we do? Shall we risk speaking to someone?"

Tom hesitated, then nodded. "If we can't see the guards, maybe they won't see us. And we have to find out where to go to find a sea serpent. Come on, we have to risk it."

Together, they scrambled down onto the shore, the shingle crunching under their feet. The fishermen looked up, peering through the mist.

"Good morning," one said, touching his flat cap.

"And to you," Quinn said. "How goes the fishing?"

The old man shrugged. "What fishing? You think we can take the boats out in this weather? Never seen mist like this before."

"It's strange, isn't it?" Quinn said. "How long has it been hanging around like this?"

"I guess it's been nigh on three weeks," the fisherman said, after a long pause. "Ever since the night of the dark moon."

Quinn and Tom exchanged swift glances. Lord Mortlake had attacked Wolfhaven Castle on the night of the dark moon. It seemed the heavy mist of that night had never gone away.

"Lucky the lord has had so much work on," the fisherman went on. "Most of the young folk have gone into town to earn what they can. The lord's being right generous, so hopefully none will starve come this winter."

"The lord?" Tom asked.

The fisherman squinted at him. "Aye. Lord Wolfgang. Lord of the castle. How is it you don't know of him?"

"I . . . I thought he . . . he was not here." Tom was utterly bewildered, but thought it best to find out exactly what was going on.

The fisherman laughed. "The lord is not one for gallivanting around, lad. He's not left his castle since his dear lady died. That was a sad day, it's true, but close on five years have passed and it's good to see the lord has recovered his spirits at last."

Tom and Quinn were stunned into silence. Luckily, the fisherman was happy to chat and went on without any prompting.

"Maybe it's because his daughter is to be married. A wedding's just the thing to cheer an old man up."

"A wedding?" Quinn asked.

"Aye. His daughter. Lady Elanor, her name is."

"Lady Elanor is to be married?" Tom had a creeping sense of unreality, as if he and Quinn had wandered through the mist into a different place or time.

"She's to marry Lord Cedric, the son of the Lord of Frostwick Castle. Any day now. The lord's busy having the castle redecorated. New tapestries for all the walls and new silver plates for the wedding guests to eat from. My son tells me there's a new cart trundling up the hill every minute, coming from Crowthorne Castle, just laden with treasures." The fisherman had a look of wonderment on his face.

"From Crowthorne Castle?" Quinn exchanged a startled look with Tom.

"Yes. The old lady there has announced Lord Cedric Mortlake as her heir. Not having a son of her own, you know."

Tom could only stare at the old man in utter amazement. Lady Ravenna of Crowthorne Castle was a miserly old bat. She would never send cartloads of treasure to anyone.

"They say Lady Ravenna is sick unto death, and fretting about having no heir. Lady Mortlake has been there, nursing her, and Lady Ravenna saw her fine upstanding son and declared him her heir," the old man went on. "She's signed everything over to him!"

Tom had an image of Cedric as he had last seen him, a weedy, anxious-faced boy shoveling food into his mouth as fast as he could. It seemed so unlike the shrewd, sharp-eyed Lady Ravenna to pass control of all her lands to a boy like that. *She must have been put under some kind of spell by Lady Mortlake*, Tom thought. Which meant there was no hope of help from that quarter now or in the future.

Tom's heart sank as he realized just how alone he and his friends were.

"Lord Wolfgang's been busy building a grand new fleet of ships too," the fisherman went on. "I wish he'd throw some of that money our way, so we could repair our boats, but that's lords for you, they never think of the simple folk."

"What does he want a new fleet for?" Tom demanded in surprise.

The fisherman spread wide his hands. "Who knows? Any other man, I'd say he was readying an army. But Lord Wolfgang is too old for such foolery. The word in the town is that the ships are a gift for Lord Mortlake, but he has no river or harbor. What use would ships be to him?"

Tom could only gape at the fisherman. Could the town and village truly not know about Lord Mortlake's invasion? How was that possible?

"Mind you, my son says it's Lord Mortlake that comes down to the harbor each day to whip the men along," the fisherman continued. "He's an impatient man, by all accounts."

"Has . . . has anyone seen Lady Elanor lately?" Quinn asked, trying to sound unconcerned.

He shrugged. "Apparently she's a shy, withdrawn thing. Her governess takes a tray up to her each day."

"Her governess?" Quinn repeated. Did that mean Mistress Mauldred had survived the invasion? The others hadn't mentioned seeing her in the dungeon when she had scried for them.

"Aye. So my daughter says. She's working in the castle kitchen now. Feasts every night!"

"What of Lord Wolfgang? Has your daughter seen him?" Tom asked.

Both shaggy gray eyebrows shot up. For the first time, the fisherman seemed to find the children's curiosity odd. "Well, no. But she's just a kitchen maid and he's the lord. I wouldn't expect her to be rubbing elbows with him."

Tom had so many other questions, but he didn't want to attract any attention. "I guess not," he quickly said. "Well, I suppose we'd better be getting on."

"We're looking for an old man I used to know," Quinn said. "He was a sailor once. He said he'd sailed all around the world."

The man's seamed face relaxed into a grin. "Ha,

that'd be old Willard you're wanting. Full of tall tales, that one. He lives in the cottage with the blue door. Talk the leg off a donkey if you let him."

"Thanks," Quinn said, and she and Tom hurried away across the shingle.

The cottage with the blue door was at the far end of the harbor, tucked right under the steep cliff of the headland. From its step, Tom could see the castle far above him, looming out of the mist. It seemed to hang over them, ready to crash down on their heads.

Quinn was white-faced, staring up at the tower. "Someone up there is looking for us," she whispered. "I can feel their eyes, searching."

"Let's get out of sight, then." Tom rapped sharply on the door.

The OLD MAN WHO SAILED AROUND THE WORLD

The man who opened the door had a bald, sun-spotted head, a flowing white beard and skin like old leather. He leaned heavily on a walking stick made of gnarled driftwood.

"Aye?" the old man asked, peering at them with faded blue eyes.

"Master Willard?" When the old man nodded, Quinn went on, "I don't know if you remember me . . . I used to come down and visit you when I was a little girl. My name is Quinn, and this is my friend Tom."

He peered at her, then his wrinkled face broke into a broad, toothless smile. "Quinn! Of course I remember you. Come in, come in," he said, ushering them inside. "I was the one that found you. Bobbing up and down in a basket on the morning tide, right outside my door. Crying your little lungs out, you were."

The cottage had only one room, but it was clean and tidy. A fire glowed on the hearth in the center of the room with a black pot hung on a tripod. A stool was set beside it, and pots and pans and spoons hung from a frame above. A neatly made bed took up one wall and a white-scrubbed table the other.

"You were so hungry, poor little thing. I brought you in and gave you some bread soaked in milk, and you gobbled it down like you'd never seen food before." He drew up some stools for them by the fire. "Talking about food, I was just about to eat. Are you hungry?"

"Starving," Tom said.

The old man's blue eyes twinkled. "Well then, sit yourself down and I'll get something for you."

Soon the small room was filled with the delicious smell of fried bacon. The old man kept chatting away about how he had taken the little foundling Quinn up to the castle and given her into the care of the Grand Teller.

"How old was I?" Quinn asked. She was sitting on the edge of her stool, her hands clasped before her, eyes fixed intently on the old man's face.

"Only a few months old. Pretty little thing, with all that dark hair and those big green eyes like the sea. All wrapped up in a lacy shawl and your clothes made of fine silk."

"Really?" Quinn's eyes widened in surprise.

"Yes. You had a most beautiful rattle tucked in with you, too. All made of silver. Arwen gave it to me as a reward. It would have fetched a pretty price if I'd sold it."

"You mean you didn't sell it?"

"Indeed, I still have it. I used to give it to you to play with when you came down to visit me. Do you remember?"

Quinn shook her head. Willard turned the sizzling bacon then hobbled across to a battered old chest under the window. After a few moments' rummaging, he shuffled back with a small tarnished rattle in his hand. At one end was a loop for a baby's hand to clutch; at the other end was a round bauble beautifully embossed with knots of ribbons and flowers and flying birds. A shield was on the bauble's front, and embossed upon it was a dove soaring high over storm clouds, three stars arching above. The dove carried a heart in its beak.

Quinn rubbed at the dove with her thumb. "I feel as though I do remember it," she said. "Just a little." She gave it a shake and the rattle tinkled musically. "It has a bell inside." She looked up, her face glowing.

Tom sat silently, watching and listening. Quinn rarely talked about being a foundling child. He had thought she did not care. But now, seeing her face as she held the baby's rattle, he realized that she cared very much indeed. He remembered how hard it had been for him, never knowing his own father. Yet Tom's mother had always been there, plump and loving and sweet smelling. He'd known where he'd come from and who he was. Quinn knew only that she'd been abandoned in a basket in the sea, at the mercy of the waves. All her life she must have wondered who had abandoned her and why . . .

"Keep it, if you like," Willard said gruffly. "It is yours, after all."

Quinn nodded her head in thanks and held the rattle close. Willard served up crispy bacon with fried laverbread made of seaweed and oatmeal. Tom and Quinn ate hungrily. The old man drank pear cider, but poured creamy goat's milk for his guests.

"Quinn says you know many great stories," Tom said, as soon as he could not dab up any more crumbs with his fingers.

"Does she? I'm glad she remembers," the old man said with a beaming smile. "Well, I've sailed all around the world, you know, and seen many marvelous things. I've seen fish as large as islands, with fountains on their heads; I've seen islands made all of ice, with dead men frozen inside them; and I've seen—"

"Have you ever seen a sea serpent?" Quinn interrupted in excitement.

"Oh, not me, no, but I've heard of a chain of islands guarded by sea serpents. It's a dreadful place, they say, haunted by ghosts and ruled over by a black witch. It was once a kingdom, but the witch caused it to flood and drown. I've heard that, on a clear day, you can look down through the water and see the towers of the castle and the roofs of the drowned town, far below the surface. And that is where the sea serpents live, in that drowned kingdom."

"That's so sad," Quinn whispered.

"Where is it?" Tom asked.

"Well, that I can tell you." The old sailor took a deep draught from his ceramic mug and settled back to tell his tale. "Once, long ago, I was sailing on a merchant ship out of Wolfhaven Castle and we were swept away in a storm. Far out to sea we were blown, for a day and a night. Then—when we were many miles from any shore—I heard the strangest thing I've ever heard in my life." The old man leaned forward and lowered his voice. "I heard bells ringing."

For a moment he was silent, his hands clenched around his mug, then he sat back.

"I have never seen men so frightened as that crew. 'The bells, the bells,' they all cried, and fell to their knees and prayed to the gods of the sea to spare them.

"But the captain would not let them fall into despair. 'I refuse to die this day!' he shouted. 'Sail, boys, sail like you've never sailed before!' So we all heaved to and worked those sails and that tiller, and we rode right into the teeth of that storm to try and get away from those ringing bells. When at last the wind died and the waves eased, we found ourselves very far from home but grateful to be alive. That was when the captain told me the story of the drowned kingdom. When you hear the bells, he said, it means you sail among the Cursed Islands where the sea serpents live. No one can survive those seas, for those great scaly beasts coil around your ship and *crush* it to splinters."

Tom and Quinn sat silently, filled with trepidation. The old man's tale made their quest seem even more impossible than ever.

"Has anyone ever tamed a sea serpent?" Quinn asked timidly.

The old man stared at her in astonishment. "No. And I can't think why anyone would want to."

"Where exactly did you hear the bells?" Tom asked. As the old man turned his startled blue eyes towards him, Tom added quickly, "So we can make sure we stay well away."

Willard stumped over to his sea chest and searched through it for a large, rolled up map. He unfurled it on the table and Tom and Quinn leaned over it as the old man weighed down the curling corners with his mug, a shell and a jar of pickled herring.

"Here," the old man said, and put his squat finger down right in the midst of the blue expanse of the sea. "They are called the Lost Isles by some, but cursed

The Cursed Isles

To Frostwick

E

W

S

they are and the Cursed Isles they shall always be to me."

Quinn held the rattle, warm in her hands, and stared at the archipelago Willard was pointing to. *Now we just need to find ourselves a boat,* she thought to herself.

THE
COFFIN MAKERS

As Quinn led the way out of the old fisherman's cottage, the rolled up map under Tom's arm, she saw something through the drifting mist that made her heart bound with unexpected joy.

Beached on the shingle, only a few paces away, was a boat.

It had been painted with round golden eyes on either side of the prow, which had been carved to look like an owl's beak.

"Owl-Eyes!" Quinn exclaimed. "Look, Tom. It's Arwen's boat!"

He stopped in his tracks. "How did it get here? It wasn't here half an hour ago!"

Quinn smiled. The last time she'd seen the Grand Teller's boat, it had been resting on a bank under a willow tree at Frostwithy Falls, near Frostwick Castle, the home of Lord Mortlake and his family. The waterfall was several hours' sail up the river from Wolfhaven Castle and its sea harbor. Yet here the boat was, just when they needed one so desperately.

Willard hobbled out after them. "She's a nice looking boat," he said appreciatively. "Lovely lines." Leaning heavily on his stick, he limped down to the seashore and examined her closely. "Interesting. Never seen a boat made all of rowan before."

Quinn said nothing, but her skin tingled as she ran her hand along the carved prow. Rowan was a magical tree; its wood offered protection from dark magic. It did not surprise her at all to find out that Owl-Eyes was made out of rowan wood.

The old man said his farewells and stumped back to his cottage. Tom and Quinn were left staring at the beached boat.

"It looks bigger than I remember it," said Quinn. "Big enough for all of us and the creatures, now, too."

Tom looked at her wonderingly. "Could the Grand Teller have sent it?"

Quinn shook her head. "She's still in the dungeon. She would have no way of knowing where we are." She stroked the prow again. "But she may have enchanted it when we first left Wolfhaven. I think it's followed us here."

"Should we sail it around to meet the others, or go and get everyone and come back here?" Tom asked.

"This is the only safe harbor for miles," Quinn replied. "There's nowhere we could pick them up. No, we'll have to bring them here."

"It'll take a while," Tom said, frowning. "And we'll have to be careful not to be seen."

"We still have to buy supplies, too," Quinn said.

"By the sounds of it, no one in the town knows anything about Lord Mortlake's attack, so it should be safe to go and buy some food at the market." Tom frowned. "It's all just so strange!" he burst out. "How could nobody realize? The castle is attacked, and all the castle folk killed or imprisoned, and yet life goes on as normal with no one noticing!"

"It's some kind of magic." Quinn rubbed her arms. "My skin is all numb and tingly, and my thumbs are twitching. Something wicked is happening here. I wish I knew exactly what . . ." Her voice died away.

"Well, all we can do is carry on. How about you go into town and get the food, and I go and fetch the others?" Tom said. "I can call Rex to come and get me once I'm out of sight of the castle. We'll meet you back on the beach."

Quinn agreed, though the idea of going into the town unnerved her. Tom gave her his bag of coins and together they dragged Owl-Eyes farther up the beach so she would not drift away on the tide. Then the two friends hurried back up the beach and climbed the stairs, parting at the path that led away into the forest.

As Quinn walked, she slipped her hand in her pocket to touch the small silver rattle that Willard had given to her. It chimed gently. She had to admit the knowledge of it warmed her. Would someone carelessly abandoning a baby wrap her in a soft shawl and give her a favorite toy to play with? It gave Quinn hope that perhaps she had not been dumped because no one wanted her, but for some other unfathomable reason.

She reached the curve of the castle rock. Below, the valley was filled with fog. Quinn could only see the vague shape of buildings and, in the distance, the arches of the bridge across the harbor. A rhythmic banging noise was so muffled by the mist it was hard to tell from which direction it came. As Quinn wandered down the steps into the town, the fog wrapped around her. She shivered.

Everyone she passed walked very slowly, their heads bowed and their shoulders hunched. No one paid her any attention at all. It was as if she was a ghost, walking through a town full of ghosts. The market stalls were open, but nobody shouted out their wares or offered her a free bite. Nobody commented on the weather, or whistled at their work. When Quinn mentioned the mist, they all just shrugged.

As Quinn went from stall to stall, buying bread from the baker; bacon, sausages and pork pies from the butcher; and pears and apples from the fruit-monger, she asked innocent-sounding questions about what was going on up in the castle. Everyone was mildly pleased about the upcoming marriage of Lady Elanor and Lord Cedric. No one thought it was strange that nobody had seen Elanor in weeks. No one wondered why it was Lord Mortlake issuing orders in the shipbuilders' yards, instead of Lord Wolfgang. All their voices were toneless, their faces blank.

It was all very odd, but the thought soon drifted out of Quinn's mind. She felt so tired, and all the supplies were so very heavy. Her head ached and her chest hurt when she breathed. She thought longingly of her little bed in the Grand Teller's tree, with its white, feather-stuffed eiderdown. How she wished she could just lie down and sleep! If only she could lie down, just for a moment.

Quinn found herself swaying on her feet. She shifted the bulging pack to her other shoulder and put out one hand to steady herself against the wall. She could see no more than a few paces ahead of her. All the shops had lit their lanterns, even though it was the middle of the day. Their glow was diffused like a fuzzy head of dandelion seeds. Quinn leaned against the wall. She was so tired. If only she could rest a moment.

Wake up, little maid, wake up. Thou art ensorcelled.

Sylvan's voice roused her. Quinn jerked her head up. She had no idea where she was. She stumbled along the street, trying to peer through the mist. She felt so strange and sick, and her legs were wobbly. The mist parted to show the dark opening of a narrow alleyway. Quinn crept inside.

Run from here, little maid, Sylvan said. *Run as fast and as far as thou can.*

But the words barely pierced the fog in her brain. Quinn's legs were trembling so much, she let herself slide down and sit on a step. Shivers ran over her. Quinn wrapped her shawl around her, trying to warm herself. She could see nothing but mist, hear nothing but mist.

Sleep . . . a voice said in her mind.

Quinn leaned her head against the stone.

Sleep . . .

A burning warmth on her chest woke her. It was the Oak King. *Wake, little maid, wake!* Sylvan's voice was hoarse and desperate. *Wake, else thou shalt die!*

Quinn tried to rouse herself, but it was like struggling up from a pit of treacle. Just opening her eyes took tremendous effort. She tried to move, but her arms and legs were limp and heavy. Somehow she managed to heave up one cold, numb hand and cup the oak medallion. Its warmth gave her strength. She lifted her head and looked around.

The cobblestones drifted away into white vapor under the blurred glow of the lanterns. Quinn had an uneasy feeling that a great deal of time had passed. Everything was dim and gloomy, as if dusk was falling.

Lamb brain, she chided herself.

Thou were ensorcelled, Sylvan told her again. *The whole town is ensorcelled. This mist is an evil vapor. It slows the heart and numbs the mind. Thou must escape before it casts its shadowy web over thee again.*

Quinn clambered to her feet. She was stiff and sore. She tried to remember where she was, but the hours before she had fallen asleep seemed like a terrible nightmare.

Then she heard the tramp of marching feet. Quinn

pressed herself against the wall. She heard knocking on a door, then a man's voice apologizing.

"I'm sorry to disturb you, sir. We're looking for a raggedy-looking girl with green eyes and long, dark curly hair. She's been accused of stealing. Have you seen her? No? I see. If you do, please raise the hue and cry. Thank you."

Quinn heard the door shut, then another door being knocked upon and opened. She crept to the mouth of the alley and looked out. The street beyond was full of soldiers, all dressed in the familiar green jerkin with the wolf head insignia of Elanor's family. None of the faces were familiar to her, though. They were hard-faced strangers, heavily armed, disguised in the clothes of the castle men-at-arms.

Who was after her?

Quinn didn't know what to do. If they saw her, she would be caught. She crept away down the alley and found herself in a courtyard lined with big double doors. The mist oozed in eddies above the small square of cobbles, but only wisps of it moved down into the courtyard. Her head began to clear as the tramp of boots behind her sent her scuttling through one door which had been propped open with a stone.

Inside were rows and rows of long wooden boxes. Quinn stopped short, aghast, realizing they were coffins. Only then did she see two men, working away at the far end of the room. She crept under a black-painted cart bearing a coffin, which stood near the open door, and hid beneath its shadows just in time. The soldiers banged at the door and barked out their question once again.

"No, sir," one of the coffin makers answered. "We've not seen any such girl."

"There's a reward for her capture," one of the soldiers said.

"We'll turn her in if we find her," the coffin makers promised.

The soldiers marched away, but the coffin makers were standing right next to the cart, talking in low voices.

"Always poking and prying their long noses into other people's business," the younger one complained. "Lord Wolfgang never used to be such a busybody. You can hardly scratch yourself these days without a soldier wanting to know if you were bitten by a flea or by a louse."

"Don't complain," the older man said. "Business has never been so good. We'll get rich if this goes on."

"But what does he want all these coffins for?" the younger man wanted to know. "I heard from the blacksmith's boy that he's been busy forging swords and cannonballs. Why? What does Lord Wolfgang plan?"

"Shhh," the other man cautioned him. "Don't say a word. Tittle-tattlers end up in one of these." He knocked on the coffin on the cart.

A bell tolled out, deep and melancholy.

"Time for evensong," the older man said. "Let's go."

The two men harnessed an old black cart horse to the hearse and guided it out of the warehouse and down the alleyway. Quinn had taken the chance to scramble up next to the coffin and crouch under the filmy black hearse cloth. She peered out through its folds and saw that the twilight streets were full of soldiers, knocking on doors, hurling aside piles of boxes and barrels, poking their pikes into heaps of straw. Somebody wanted to find her very badly.

The hearse rumbled through the town, heading towards the graveyard. Quinn was bumped and bruised with every rut and pothole. It was almost dark. How long had she been asleep? Would her friends be searching for her?

As the hearse rolled through the gates of the grave-yard, Quinn slipped down. The laden pack banging on her shoulders, she scurried into the shadows cast by the dark yew trees, then made her way stealthily towards the steps that led towards the fishing village.

"There she is!" a cry rang out. "Stop, thief!"

Quinn broke into a run. Down the steep, uneven stone steps she bolted, not turning to see how many chased her, scarcely able to catch her breath.

Soldiers pounded after her. Quinn ran as fast as she could, but the mist weighed down her arms and legs and lungs. A stitch stabbed her side.

Somebody grabbed at her arm, but she wrested herself free and ran on. She could hear the steady beat of running feet, the pant of breath, the quick snapped order: "Stop her! Bring her down!"

7

»→OWL-EYES←«

A ray of silvery blue light illuminated Quinn. She gasped and slowed.

Then a long, gray shape sprang out of the darkness, bringing a soldier down with a crash on the cobblestones. "Fergus!" Quinn panted.

The next moment, a unicorn galloped out of the mist. Elanor rode on his back, one hand held high as if she carried a sword. The Traveler's Stone shone from it, and she wielded it like a lance, blinding the soldiers who sought to drag Quinn down. The unicorn slashed from side to side with his long horn. Fergus leaped and snarled and dragged down another soldier.

One man was beside her, determined to grab her,

but then an arrow whizzed through the air and caught him in the shoulder. Quinn looked up and saw Tom hovering right above her on the griffin's back, firing a frenzy of arrows.

A small dragon swooped through the air, spitting flames. Arrows hissed. The wolf cub snapped at a soldier's ankles and caused him to trip and fall with a clatter of armor on stone. The griffin shrieked in rage. Then Sebastian leaped from the darkness and caught Quinn's hand. "Run!"

Hand in hand with Sebastian, Quinn ran as she had never run before. Fergus loped ahead of her, lunging at anyone who tried to stop them. Together Elanor and Tom and their beasts fought behind them, keeping the soldiers back. The beat of the griffin's wings made the suffocating mist swirl and part. Fresh sea air blew in their faces. Quinn felt a sudden quickening of her senses. Only then did she realize how dazed she had been.

Down the stairs Quinn ran, with the clatter of the unicorn's hooves behind her. She saw a red-streaked sky ahead of them and the shimmer of the dusk-colored waters. They tumbled down the steps and onto the sandy shingle . . . and there was Owl-Eyes, patiently waiting for them.

She and Sebastian scrambled onto the boat. Fergus leapt after them. Sebastian grabbed Wulfric by the scruff of his neck and hauled him aboard. Beltaine flew to his shoulder, hiccupping sparks.

Quickthorn galloped towards them, Elanor crouched low on his back. Behind them ran what seemed like hundreds of soldiers, all shouting and shaking their pikes. Sebastian used the oar to push them into the harbor. The unicorn leapt across the widening expanse of water and landed on Owl-Eyes' deck, all four hooves skidding as he tried to slow himself. Quinn hauled on the sail which bellied out in the breeze. The boat rocked as Rex dropped out of the sky like a ton of gold. Tom dropped and rolled and came up firing, while the griffin soared away again, shrieking with triumph.

Owl-Eyes flung itself onto the quickening tide. The soldiers were left behind on the shore, helplessly shouting and raging.

Swiftly the rowan boat was swept towards the harbor entrance. Spray flew in their faces. Sebastian spluttered and spat. Then the four friends jumped up and down, cheering.

"What can be swallowed but also swallow you?" Quinn said, as quick as a whip.

"Quinn! You'll jinx us!" Elanor cried.

"Why? What's the answer?" said Sebastian. "What does she mean?"

"Water!" Tom answered, sweeping one hand out to show Sebastian the wild ocean crashing beyond the headlands. The sea was foaming white among the black rocks, throwing spray up like fountains.

Sebastian fixed Quinn with a furious glance. "Bad joke, Quinn!"

She shrugged with a rueful smile. Next moment, her face shadowed. She clutched Elanor's arm, pointing with her other hand. "Look!"

A figure stood in the window of the highest tower of the castle, which rose from the mist like a needle thrust into gray silk. It was a woman, by the bell-shape of her skirts. Both arms were flung high.

Quinn heard an eerie voice . . . "*I see you. I know you.*" Pain overcame her and she fell to her knees. She pressed her fingers to her temples.

"That's my governess, Mistress Mauldred!" Elanor said in a wondering voice. "But—"

"Really? Are you sure?" Tom demanded, as he helped Quinn to her feet.

Elanor nodded. "I'm certain of it. I'd recognize her figure anywhere!"

The mist swirled apart. Wind roared and huge waves bucked. Owl-Eyes was swept with a rush of black water towards the rocks.

"It's her that's doing this!" Quinn shouted, pointing up to the figure in the tower. "She's the one conjuring the storm!"

"But . . . how? Mistress Mauldred's a witch?" Elanor asked in astonishment.

"A very powerful one," Quinn gasped, staggering with the pain in her head. "She's trying to sink us!"

Lightning struck. Thunder cracked. High above, they heard the griffin shriek, but he was lost to sight in the tumbling maelstrom of storm clouds. Black, foam-streaked waves reared high on all sides. Quinn stumbled forward. She grasped the oak medallion tightly in one hand and drew strength from it. "Quick, we need to bring Owl-Eyes around," she gasped. "Tom, grab that rope and pull on it hard. Sebastian, you take the tiller. Keep her headed straight towards the middle of the harbor entrance. Ela, you'll need to tie the animals up, else they'll be swept overboard."

Everyone quickly obeyed. Quinn gripped tight to the mast. "Come on, Owl-Eyes, you can do it," she urged over the scream of the witch wind.

The boat heeled over, the sail swinging across with a great *thwack*. Tom ducked, the boom missing him by a whisker. Owl-Eyes swerved and straightened. It seemed to leap from wave to wave, spray gushing up on either side. Quinn felt her stomach drop and heave, and took a deep breath, hanging on with all her strength.

She stared up at the tower. Black, anvil-shaped clouds loomed behind the tower. Although Mistress Mauldred was just a dark shape against the lit window, Quinn could feel her gaze boring into her.

The governess flung up her arms once more and a red light glinted sharply from her fingers. Again the wind gusted, almost capsizing the little boat. The children flung their weight to the other side, trying to keep Owl-Eyes afloat, but the boat spun out of control. Working desperately, they managed to bring it around once more and it raced out between the rocks and into the open sea.

Thunder clapped overhead. Lightning flashed so close, everyone screamed. The air smelled like firework smoke. Quinn coughed, her eyes stinging. Rain pelted down on them, as cold as ice. Hail began to batter the deck. Quickthorn reared and plunged, fighting to be free of the rope that bound him.

They all looked back at the tower, but it was obscured now in heavy, roiling clouds. The hail clattered on the deck, lumps of ice as large as rocks. Everyone ducked down, shielding their faces as best they could. The wind tore at the sails.

"We need to reef the sails," Quinn called. "Help me, Tom. Sebastian, bring the boat about, head it into the wind. Ela, ease that rope a little. Be careful! Tom, help me! We have to bring the sails halfway down the mast. Don't let the rope run free!"

Lightning flashed again, striking the water close by the hull, blindingly brilliant. Sebastian let go of the tiller to shield his eyes and Owl-Eyes lurched away. The clap of thunder was so loud it deafened them all, leaving their ears ringing.

Tom dragged on the rope with all his strength and brought the flapping sail under control. Sebastian seized the tiller again. Boldly, the little boat climbed up, up, up the slope of the wave, teetered for a moment on its rushing crest, then plunged down, down, down. Quinn's stomach dropped with it. Her feet left the deck. For a heart-stopping moment, she thought she would fly up into the air, the boat falling away below her. Then the boat began to climb again, foam cascading down the decks.

"Lash yourselves to the mast!" she called.

Tom and Elanor hurried to obey. Sebastian could not leave the tiller, his muscles bulging as he fought to keep the boat from foundering. The girls tied him to the rudder post. A wave broke on the boat and rushed down the deck, sweeping Elanor's feet out from under her. With a scream, she was dragged towards the guardrail. Tom caught her arm seconds before she was thrown overboard. With Quinn's help, he hauled her back on board and together they tied her to the mast, their fingers so stiff and numb with cold and shock they could scarcely manage to tie the knots.

Darkness had fallen. Quinn could see nothing but the spray of white foam, the curl of a breaking crest moments before it crashed upon them.

Up, up, up.

Down, down, down, down.

Would Owl-Eyes make it through the night?

8

BELLS FROM »———→
←« THE DEEP

*T*o *live in the face of certain death is a truly marvelous
thing*, Elanor thought.

She tipped back her head and looked at the sky
above her. The night drew up her black skirts, showing
a deep ruffle of red petticoat. The bright-edged stars
were folded away, leaving just one, glinting like a
diamond brooch.

Moment by moment, the sky above her and the
sea around her were changing. Crimson softened to
rose, purple faded to violet, then to lilac, and then to
the palest blue, as delicate as a finch's egg. To the east
were flecks of bright cloud like the scales of a great
golden fish. Then the sun lifted above the horizon.

A symphony of color spread from the height of the sky to the depths of the sea. Elanor wanted to sing, or shout, or kneel and weep.

She had thought she would never see such beauty again. It made her feel as if all things were possible. Magic was possible, and love, and goodness, and hope, and triumph over evil. All the things she had thought lost and forsaken in the dark horror of their night on the sea, and the dreadful realization that her governess was a traitor.

Quinn knelt beside her, eyes as green as the curve of the wave, her black hair in a wild tangle down her back. She was shivering, the wind cold on her wet clothes, but she was smiling. "Doesn't it make you feel alive? Almost dying, I mean?"

Elanor nodded.

"Not dying makes me hungry," Sebastian said. He sat hunched by the tiller, his fingers still clamped tightly around it. His wet curls dripped in his eyes. "Do you think we could eat something? Did you manage to get any food, Quinn, before you decided to take a nap back there?"

Quinn scowled at him. "I did. But it's only food for nice people."

He gave a stilted grin. "Sorry. I am nice, I promise. I was only joking."

Quinn relented and scrambled over to the cupboard where she had stowed all their supplies. Thankfully the cupboard was watertight, so they were able to enjoy a feast of soft white bread with butter and honey, small crisp apples with shiny red skin and flesh as white as snow, and lemon balm tea made with fresh rainwater heated on Owl-Eyes' little stove.

"This is the best meal I've ever had," Tom said. Fergus whined and put one heavy paw on his leg, so Tom cut him a slice of curling pink ham. At once, Wulfric put his paw on Tom's other leg, head tilted, eyes imploring. Tom sighed and cut him a slice, then returned his gaze to the sea. His brow was furrowed.

"What's wrong?" Quinn asked.

"I'm worried about Rex. It's been hours since we last saw him." Tom dug out his elder wood flute. He began to play a haunting tune, the notes soaring out across the water into the dawn-fresh wind.

Before long, the flute song was answered by a high sharp call. Far, far above, golden feathers flashed and the griffin came circling down. He had a limp, gray-feathered seabird clasped in one talon and tossed it down to the deck before landing gracefully in the bow. The boat dipped dangerously low.

"Thanks, Rex," Tom said and began plucking the bird for Fergus and Wulfric. Quickthorn, meanwhile, was munching his way through the bundle of wild grasses that Elanor had gathered for him. "I hope he doesn't eat it all now," Elanor said. "Who knows when we'll see land again."

This thought sobered them all.

"Any idea where we are?" Sebastian asked.

"According to the map Willard gave us, we should sail due west if we want to find the drowned kingdom," Tom said. "The sun is right behind us so we're on track."

Elanor looked back. The rising sun made it look as if they were sailing on a river of golden fire. The warmth on her back felt wonderful.

"How long to get there?" Sebastian grabbed another crisp red apple and bit into it with relish.

"I don't know . . . but Willard said his ship was blown there by a storm in a night and a day from Wolfhaven Harbor so hopefully that is how long it will take us, too," Quinn replied.

"The problem with being at sea is there are no landmarks," Elanor said, shading her eyes to stare out at the blue horizon.

"The land that never changes and never stills," Quinn said. "Plowed by travelers far from home, but never planted."

"Another riddle?" Tom sighed.

She laughed with delight. "Riddle me ree, the riddler, that's me!"

Beltaine woke and flew around the boat, croaking damp squibs of sparks. She didn't like the water much, until she realized that fish swam in its depths. Then she tried to catch them and grew quite adept, swooping down, seizing them from the waves and then flipping them up in the air to catch. Sebastian coaxed her to drop a few on the boat and Tom fried them up for lunch. "She's turning into quite a useful little dragon," Sebastian said.

"Not so little anymore," Quinn said. "I'm fairly sure she's bigger already."

Indeed, the dragon was now the size of a fully grown cat.

The wind was blowing so strong and steady from the east, the children had little to do but keep the tiller steady. "We're lucky," Sebastian said. "Normally the wind blows from the west. Sir Kevyn says that's why Wolfhaven Castle was built with so many towers and gatehouses facing the sea, as that's where the danger normally lies. That's why we always have to be on guard from invasion from the lands that way."

Quinn looked up. "You mean this wind is unusual?"

Sebastian shrugged. "I don't know. I'm a knight, not a sailor. I just know it normally blows west to east."

Quinn looked back at their wake, straight as an arrow shooting from the east. "You're right, Sebastian. It's an enchanted wind," she said with absolute conviction. "All morning I've been wondering why I feel so strange and shivery. I thought it was the aftereffects of that horrible mist and the storm, and being so cold and frightened. But it's the wind."

Elanor bit her lip. "Is it still Mistress Mauldred?"

Quinn nodded. "I think so."

"I never liked that mean woman," Tom said.

Elanor nodded. It was true. Her governess had been cruel. "But she's been with us since I was a baby. I can't believe she betrayed us."

Quinn's expression was intent. "When did she first come to the castle?"

"I don't remember . . ." Elanor fondled the wolfhound's soft ears and he laid his shaggy gray head on her knee with a sigh. "Well, my father told me once how she'd come to Wolfhaven the week before I was due to be born. It was a wild and snowy night, and she came seeking shelter. There had been some kind of storm . . . or a shipwreck. My mother fell ill . . . I came early . . . and my mother almost died. But Mistress Mauldred stayed with her all night. Everyone thought nothing could save her . . . but my mother survived."

Quinn frowned. "Maybe she saved her with witchcraft, to get in your father's good graces."

"Maybe she made your mam sick in the first place," Tom said.

Elanor wrapped her knees in her arms. "Maybe . . . I don't know. I'm just realizing that I know barely anything about her. Where she came from, whether she has any family. She never spoke about herself."

Her governess had never said anything, other than orders: *Ladies never interrupt their elders. Ladies do not speak unless spoken to. Ladies must not slouch!*

Elanor sighed.

"When did your mother die?" Sebastian asked, sympathy warm in his voice.

"When I was eight. She was always sick, but she tried not to let me see." Elanor rested her chin on her knees. Fragments of memories came to her, making her stomach knot with anxiety. "I don't think my mother liked Mistress Mauldred much."

"Why?" Sebastian asked. When Elanor glanced at him in surprise, he went on, "I mean, why do you think that? What did she do?"

"Mistress Mauldred was always trying to make me leave my mother alone and my mother was always telling her to let me stay, that she liked me there. And once Mistress Mauldred brought my mother medicine to drink, and after she'd gone, my mother made a face and tipped it into a vase of flowers, and said she hoped it wouldn't kill them . . ."

There was a long silence. Everyone looked troubled and afraid. Suddenly Elanor burst out, "I'll tell you something else. After my mother died, I woke one night so sad and scared. And I went to find my father. He was awake, he never slept in those days. He was sitting in his chair by the fire and Mistress Mauldred was there with him. She was kneeling and she had hold of his hand."

Elanor looked around at her friends. "She was gripping his hand so tight and my father was trying to draw away. It was awful. I couldn't go in. My father was asking her to let him go, saying that such a thing could never be . . . I went back to bed. I heard her coming back soon after and she was in such a rage. Doors banging, metal clanging. I thought . . . I hoped . . . oh, how I hoped she'd go away. But she didn't."

"I remember when your mam died," Tom said. "Everything changed after that. Your dad became so listless and nothing seemed to matter to him anymore."

"He was enchanted," Quinn burst out. "Of course he was! It seems so obvious when I think about it now. He was like a completely different man!"

"Do you think it's true?" cried Elanor. "Do you think he really was enchanted?" She tried to wipe away her tears, but they came too fast. "Because . . . because—oh, that would make me so relieved! I mean, no, that's stupid. I don't mean that. But to know that it wasn't my fault . . . to know that there was another reason for why he changed so much . . ."

Quinn seized her hand. "We know what you mean. That awful mist was enchanted, too." She looked over at Tom. "That must be why no one has found out what's truly happening in the castle. The townsfolk have been enchanted. When I was in town, breathing in the mist, I felt all strange and unsteady and . . . and heavy. Like my limbs were chained down. Maybe your father's been chained down all these years and no one knew it, Elanor!"

"How did I not realize?" Elanor's tears came faster. "What can we do? We have to break her spell on my father! We have to set him free!"

Sebastian looked very serious. "It all makes sense now. Mistress Mauldred must be the traitor. She conjured the mist and raised the portcullis for Lord Mortlake's men. She must have been working for him for a long time. Preparing and planning."

Elanor wiped her face with her sleeve. "But why? How does she even know him?"

"Maybe she's angry your father wouldn't marry *her* after your mother died," Quinn said.

Elanor thought about this and then nodded her head slowly. "Yes. Maybe. But it seems a cruel and cold revenge . . . and to wait so many years?"

Tom shook his head as if bothered by flies. "We're missing something. Part of the puzzle we don't yet understand. We thought it was just Lord Mortlake, wanting Wolfhaven's lands and harbor. But it's more than that. Why did he want the unicorn? He won Wolfhaven Castle easily."

"Thanks to that traitor opening the portcullis," Sebastian said hotly. *Any slur on the Wolfhaven Castle knights was a slight on him*, Elanor thought, and she loved him for his loyalty.

"That's right. Hardly any of his men were lost. So why does he need the unicorn? He must have bigger plans than we realized."

"That's why he raised all those bog-men," Sebastian said.

"And he's building ships. And coffins ... hundreds of them!" Quinn remembered the coffin makers. "Why is he building so many?"

"What if he plans to overthrow the king?" Sebastian cried. "Remember, Ela? Lady Ravenna said Lord Mortlake was related somehow to King Gwydion, who was brother to King Ivor. Lord Mortlake wants to throw King Ivor off the throne and be king himself!"

"Yes, I remember . . ." Elanor's voice shook. This was all so frightening. Her view of the world was being shaken up and transformed into something much darker, much deadlier. "But, you know, Sebastian, I am kin to the old king too . . . and closer to the throne than Lord Mortlake."

Her friends stared at her in astonishment.

"Really?" Tom cried. "But . . . how?"

"Through my *mother*," Elanor said. "Her mother—my grandmother—was King Gwydion and King Ivor's sister. That means my mother was Prince Conway's cousin. After he and his family were lost at sea, and his younger brother, Prince Derwyn, died of illness, their uncle Ivor declared himself king. But both my mother and her cousin, Lord Mortlake, could have claimed to be heirs to the throne. King Ivor seized the throne, though, and made it very clear that he would stand for no opposition. My father swore an oath to support him; my mother was sick, and she had no desire to be queen."

Everyone was still staring at her perplexedly. Elanor said apologetically, "I know the family tree can be confusing sometimes. Basically, all you need to know is that King Ivor is my mother's uncle—"

"It's not that," Tom said. "It's that other thing you said. About Lord Mortlake."

"He's your uncle?" Quinn was utterly flabbergasted by this revelation.

"Sort of. My mother's cousin."

When everyone stared at her, openmouthed,

Elanor looked anxious. "I'm sorry. I thought everyone knew. That's also why my father would not consider a marriage with Cedric. We're related."

"You *are* heir to the throne," Sebastian said, utterly flabbergasted. "No wonder my father insisted on sending me to Wolfhaven! Ha, he's a sneaky man. He wanted me to meet you. I thought it was such an out-of-the-way place!" He shook his head in admiration.

"Well, I'm not really! Only if King Ivor dies without an heir," Elanor said, a little flushed by Sebastian's words. "He's just married again. Surely his new wife will bear him an heir?"

"That's why Lord Mortlake has been so insistent you *would* marry his son!" Tom said, marveling. "If both you and your cousin Cedric are heirs . . . married, you'd have a double claim!"

Anxiety squeezed Elanor's throat so hard she could barely breathe. "No. I don't want to rule! Too many people have died for the throne!"

She stared at them, willing them to understand. After her mother's death, her father had told her again and again, *We must not make the king angry . . . we must not make him think us anything but loyal . . . let him forget we exist . . .* He had been most anxious about it, as though terrified that King Ivor would appear without warning and take Elanor away. Elanor remembered the vague terror she always felt whenever the king's name was mentioned.

There was a long silence, broken only by the relentless rush of that enchanted wind in their ropes and sails, the relentless churn of waves beneath the hull of the boat.

Then Elanor heard a distant clangor of bells, deep and low and melancholy. She sat up and shaded her eyes with her hand, looking out at the sea in sudden unease.

Quinn leaned forward, her face pale. "What's that sound? Surely . . . surely that's . . . bells?"

Still the sound rang out, muffled and mysterious.

Bells from the deep.

9

THE CURSED ISLANDS

"To hear the drowned bells is an omen of death," Quinn said. "But it's what we came here for . . ."

"Knights don't believe in omens," Sebastian said stoutly, though he was not at all sure he believed this to be true anymore. So many strange and marvelous things had happened in the last few weeks; he was prepared to believe in the possibility of anything.

"Look!" Tom pointed. "Are those islands?"

Sebastian squinted against the glitter of the sun on the water. The horizon was sullen with clouds and it was hard to tell whether those darker bruises against the sky were islands or storm clouds.

"I think they are," Elanor said.

"We've found the Cursed Isles," Quinn said in a low voice. She looked very pale and her hands were clenched on the guardrail.

"Let's do it," Elanor said bravely. "We have to find that sea serpent scale."

Sebastian nodded. "I wonder if they shed their skins like other snakes do?" he asked. "Maybe we can find an old snakeskin somewhere. Maybe we can slip in without the sea serpents noticing us, grab an old snakeskin and slip out again."

"Maybe," Tom said. He did not sound convinced.

"I've been thinking about that," Quinn said. "If all we needed was the unicorn's horn and the griffin's feather and the dragon's tooth . . . well, why have the beasts traveled so far with us? I feel certain we need them, or they would have left us long ago."

"So we don't just need to find a scale, we need to tame the sea serpent too?" Elanor whispered. She was pale, her brows contracted into a knot.

"Yes," Quinn answered. Her hand was gripping the wooden medallion she wore around her neck. "The Oak King believes so, too."

Sebastian drew his sword and rummaged in his pack till he found his trusty whetstone. *May as well make sure my sword is sharp*, he thought. He sharpened the blade, then gave the sword a swift polish with a rag. It was a new sword, much better than his original, which had been snapped in half by the two-headed giant in the Witchwood. This sword had once belonged to the Beast of Blackmoor Bog. It was finely wrought with a hilt made of writhing dragons, and Sebastian couldn't wait to show it to his father.

Beltaine came and wound around Sebastian's leg. Sebastian rubbed between the baby dragon's two pointed ears. The little creature made a pleased humming sound.

The boat raced on before the wind, its brown sail billowing. A great dark swirl of clouds was bearing down on them from the east, a gray veil of rain between sky and sea. The sea behind was indigo gray. Ahead, the water glittered under the blazing sun sliding down in the west. Sebastian could now clearly see a chain of small, steep islands rising from the sea.

Still the drowned bells tolled out, a constant

clamor from the depths.

"Look at those weird things sticking out of the water," Tom said. "What are they?"

It was hard to see against the glare of the setting sun. Sebastian shaded his eyes. "They're tree branches. Looks like we're sailing over a dead forest!"

They all hung over the side of the boat, looking down in awe at the submerged forest spreading far and wide below them. The white branches were studded with barnacles and hung with algae which moved softly in the currents, making the forest look alive. Their roots were lost in shadows.

Quinn was at the tiller; she had to carefully maneuver Owl-Eyes in and out of the tangle of bare twigs poking up through the water. Every now and again, a branch knocked against the hull of the boat with a hollow thump.

"It's like we're flying, not sailing," Elanor said, her voice full of awe.

"Those islands must be the peaks of old mountains," Sebastian said. "Look, they form a circle."

"How did the sea rise up and drown a forest?" Tom

wondered. "Or did the land sink into the sea?"

The wind was blowing harder and harder, making the boat skip across the waves. Thunder growled.

"A storm's blowing up again," Quinn said. "Let's try and get ashore before it hits us. I don't want another night like the last!"

She guided Owl-Eyes towards a small gap in the circle of islands. As the boat sailed into a vast lagoon encircled by steep islands, Elanor gasped.

She pointed down into the water, as clear as glass. "Look!"

Far below was a sunken city, half-buried in sand. Sebastian leaned on his elbows and gazed in amazement. He could see half-ruined houses with domes and arches and towers and courtyards, all overgrown with seaweed and crusted with barnacles. Streets led to squares, lined with grand buildings with gaping doorways and broken roofs. Dead trees stood in rows, fish flickering through their stiff branches like brightly colored finches. A rusty iron swing hung from a dead tree in a park, swaying back and forth, back and forth.

"It's eerie," Quinn said. "Look, there's a carriage . . ." She paused, realizing what could have been trapped inside the submerged shape. "Did they have no warning?" she asked sadly. "They mustn't have been able to flee the rush of water."

The group was quiet as they all solemnly took in their surroundings.

"There's the castle!" Tom pointed out suddenly. "Look, there's the bell tower, too. Sail over it and maybe we'll see the bells rocking to and fro."

"I don't think I want to," Quinn replied. "Let's get ourselves safely to shore."

"I agree," said Sebastian. He peered over the side of the boat. "Look, you can see our shadow," he said. He leaned farther over, watching the boat's shadow flicker over the drowned city so many fathoms below.

Another movement caught his eye. Something swift and sinuous.

He peered closer.

His gut tightened.

It was the biggest serpent he had ever seen. Silvery brown, with a black zigzag down its back. It was swimming straight towards them.

"It's a sea serpent!" he shouted.

The sea serpent was more than three times as long as the little boat, and as thick through the body as an oak tree. It moved with astonishing speed, rippling through the water.

"Tom, take the tiller!" Quinn cried. She rushed to the prow, her hands held out towards the creature. Her face was full of eagerness. Sebastian realized that she must have been longing for the chance to meet and tame a magical beast of her own. "Look! He's so beautiful," she cried.

"His scales! Look how huge they are," Elanor said in wonderment. "They're as big as a shield!"

The sea serpent reached the boat. He reared up out of the lagoon, water cascading down his sinuous body. Quinn reached up as if to stroke his silver-and-black scales. Just a few more inches and he would be within reach.

The sea serpent suddenly struck at her with glistening fangs. Quinn flinched back and fell. The fangs just missed her. She scuttled backward, her face filled with horror. Elanor raced forward and dragged Quinn back as the sea serpent struck again, his fangs tearing two great holes in the boat's wooden deck. His slanted eyes were red and malevolent.

Sebastian drew his sword.

"Quick! Ela, take the tiller!" Tom cried. As Elanor seized the tiller, he snatched up his bow and arrows. Fergus barked wildly, as Tom shot an arrow towards the sea serpent swaying so ominously over the boat.

"There are hundreds of them!" Elanor cried. Sebastian cast a quick glance where she pointed. Sea serpents writhed up through the broken archways and battlements of the drowned castle. There were too many to count.

"We have to get to shore!" Quinn looked up at the sail. It was full-bellied, straining at the ropes. She grabbed her rowan staff and ran to the bow. She stood there, arms spread wide like a ragged figurehead, and shouted to the sky: "Winds, blow! Winds, blast! Boat, go! Boat, fast!"

The wind leaped to her command, sending Owl-Eyes skimming over the white-capped waves.

Lightning flashed down behind them and rain began to pelt down. The silvery black sea serpent was just as swift, however. It reared up out of the water, its forked tongue flicking. It struck, its fangs penetrating deep into Owl-Eyes. There was a dreadful sound of wood cracking.

Sebastian charged forward, thrusting his sword into the sea serpent's lithe body. "Valor, glory, victory!" he shouted.

At the same moment, Tom shot an arrow straight through the serpent's huge slitted eye. The snake thrashed wildly. Quickthorn reared on his hind hooves, slashing at the snake with his razor-sharp horn. The triangular head fell with a thud onto the deck, while the huge, writhing body slipped away beneath the waves.

Tom screamed.

One fang had pierced through his boot and into his foot, pinning him to the deck.

10

»—→ VENOM ←—«

Sebastian wrenched the serpent's head free from the deck and hurled it overboard.

Tom fell back, moaning.

Quinn rushed to his side, crouching over him, trying to protect him with her arms as he rocked back and forth in agony, holding his ankle.

The wind was howling now, sending Owl-Eyes racing across the waves. Spray and spitting rain drenched them all. Elanor fought to control the bucking tiller.

"Help me get Tom's boot off," Quinn gasped to Sebastian. She yanked at Tom's laces, then Sebastian hauled the boot off. They had no time to be gentle.

Tom's foot was already swelling badly. He yelled, half fainting in pain.

"I'll bind up his foot and then we have to get him ashore," said Quinn, trying not to cry. This was not how she imagined her sea serpent encounter would unfold. "I don't know what the cure is for sea serpent venom . . ."

Tom's face was white and clammy. His foot was already puffed up to three times its normal size.

Far above, Rex shrieked in distress, then plummeted down to the torn and battered deck. His lion's tail was lashing furiously and his claws were fully distended. The griffin crouched, his golden eyes fixed fiercely on Tom. Quinn tore her ragged hem into strips and rapidly bound his foot.

"I don't know what else I can do. I need the Grand Teller," she sobbed.

"Let's get to shore!" Sebastian cried. "Before the boat sinks!"

Just then, a great triangular head broke out of the racing waves, rising high on a long undulating neck. The sea serpent hissed, its cold slitted eyes fixed on the boat. Another one followed, and then another and another.

Owl-Eyes was surrounded.

"More serpents!" Elanor cried.

Sebastian grabbed his sword.

The serpents swam towards the boat, long bodies rippling from side to side. The griffin soared up into the air, then dive-bombed one of the sea serpents. His huge talons closed around its neck and body and wrenched it up out of the water. The long body whipped around. Rex flew to a high crag protruding from the water and set about tearing the giant snake to pieces, devouring it with relish.

The other sea serpents had reached the boat. They twined around it, squeezing it in their coils, striking at the children. Sebastian hacked at one with his sword and narrowly missed being bitten, thanks to Elanor whacking its head with the oar. Quickthorn slashed the head off another. It fell heavily, writhing all over the deck, smashing the guardrail and knocking Sebastian off his feet. There was no way they could hold them all back.

Then a long, high blast rang out. The sea serpents turned their great, flat heads, scanning the horizon with lidless eyes. Elanor leaned forward, her heart leaping as she saw small, round boats made of wicker racing towards them over the water. Each boat carried two passengers, one wielding oars, the other carrying a long, sharp weapon. Their scaly skin glinted silver gray, marked with black zigzags. Their hair was long and matted into elflocks, and they wore belts of braided seaweed.

"Look at those basket boats," Quinn cried. "They've come to help us!"

Each scaly warrior held a huge white shell to their lips like a trumpet, blowing into it and creating the sound that echoed all around the lagoon. Then they attacked the sea serpents with long weapons made of driftwood and seal tusks. For a while, all was wild turmoil. Sea serpents raced through the water, long bodies unspooling, wicked fangs flashing as they struck left and right. Sebastian wielded his sword with all his strength and the unicorn stabbed the glittering coils winding around the boat. The griffin soared and plunged, tearing the sea serpents apart. Elanor struck out with her dagger and Quinn laid to with the long witch's staff, even as she wiped away tears of disappointment and dismay.

The lagoon was a maelstrom of churning waves and struggling silver serpentine shapes. The shells rang out again. Then the sea serpents turned and writhed away, disappearing into the shadowy depths of the lagoon.

Sebastian leaned forward, panting, on his sword. His legs felt like jelly.

"Here, catch this!" a boy's voice rang out.

Sebastian looked over the stern. A wicker boat bobbed below, a boy holding a coil of rope in his hands. He flung one end up to Sebastian. "We'll tow you to shore," the boy cried. "The sea serpents have retreated for now, but they will come back so we need to be quick. Hang on and we'll haul you to safety."

The griffin swooped down, and the boy's eyes widened. "Is that . . . what is that?"

"A griffin," Sebastian said.

Elanor flapped her hands at Rex. "Go, Rex, go!

Out of sight!"

The griffin soared away. The boy watched him go, mouth open in amazement.

Other wicker boats bumped all around Owl-Eyes and more ropes were tossed up. Sebastian tied them to the guardrail around the broken bow. The oarsmen all rowed furiously and the battered boat was slowly dragged to the shore of one of the islands.

There was no beach, only rocks sharp with oyster shells and barnacles lying just underneath the water. The shallow-bottomed wicker boats skimmed lightly over the top, but Owl-Eyes was too large. They maneuvered her into a channel of deeper water and dropped the anchor. Their rescuers swarmed up and into the boat, lifting a fainting Tom and lowering him carefully into one of the wicker boats.

"We'll do what we can for him," one of the men said, his face grave.

Elanor and Quinn clung to each other. Fergus whined pitifully, and Sebastian tried to comfort him, a hard lump in his throat. Two strong men hoisted the boat up, Tom lying senseless inside.

All the other wicker boats were hoisted high too, flipped upside down, and then carried onto the shore. "Get what you need and come ashore," said the boy.

Sebastian stared at him in amazement. He was around the same age as Sebastian and his friends, with long dark hair that stuck out in a multitude of thick matted elflocks, decorated with tiny feathers and shells. His skin was silvery and scaly, except for his face, which was brown and smiling. From his seaweed belt hung his conch shell horn, a dagger made of some kind of bone and a long curved sword. Sebastian had never seen a weapon like it. Made of driftwood, its edges were studded with sharp white sharks' teeth and a seal's curving tusk was bound to the tip. Sebastian would have loved a chance to practice a few swings with it.

The boy, meanwhile, was staring in amazement at Quickthorn. The unicorn was restless and uneasy, tossing his horned head and stamping around on his black hooves. There was no way to conceal him.

"Is that a unicorn?" The boy's voice was filled with astonished disbelief.

"Yep," Sebastian replied nonchalantly.

"But don't go near him!" Elanor cried. "He . . . he doesn't like strangers."

Quickthorn was sweeping the air with his horn, nostrils flaring.

"Keep back!" the boy called to his people. "Can someone go and fetch the ramp? We'll need it to get him off."

Sebastian had shouldered his and Tom's packs and came across to give Elanor hers. Beltaine had crept inside his jacket at the sight of all the strangers, but now she peeked her red-horned head out, blue eyes wide and inquisitive.

"And is that a *dragon?*" the boy said.

"Yep," Sebastian said again, then added, "she's only a baby. She'll grow much bigger."

"How big?" the boy wanted to know.

Sebastian thought of the dragon skeleton that he had ridden from the bog to the cliffs. "Big," he answered and tucked the little beast back protectively inside his jacket.

Quinn came towards them, her skirt in tatters

from where she had torn it to make bandages, her hair blowing everywhere in the gusting wind. Her eyes were the exact color of the lagoon behind her. "Thank you for coming to our rescue. We'd never have been able to fight off those sea serpents without you."

"You were lucky our lookout saw you," the boy answered. "The serpents are deadly fast."

She nodded. "I'm Quinn, and this is Sebastian and Elanor. Our friend who is hurt is Tom." She shaded her eyes, watching as the boat in which Tom lay was carried gently to shore.

"I'm Finn," the boy answered. "Welcome to Willowmere."

Fergus was whining in distress, his paws up on the guardrail, his brown eyes scanning the shore anxiously. Beside him, the fluffy little wolf cub tried to put his paws up too, but his legs were too short and so he bounced, yapping shrilly.

Finn's eyes widened. "Is that—" he began, but then bit off the end of his sentence.

Sebastian grinned. "Yep." He was actually starting to enjoy this.

"A wolf cub? On a boat? With a wolfhound?"

"It's a long story."

"I'd like to hear it," Finn said. "Come, let's get you to safety. That witch storm is still brewing."

Sebastian looked up at the sky. It was black and scarlet, clawed with gold. Thunder rumbled ominously.

The other warriors had returned with a wooden ramp that they heaved up to the side of the boat. Elanor was able to lead Quickthorn down the ramp and onto the rocky shore. The unicorn's eyes were rolling white and he flared his nostrils at the scent of all the strangers. "Is there somewhere quiet and safe and away from people I can take him?" she asked Finn anxiously. "He's still very skittish after facing those sea serpents. I wouldn't want him to hurt anyone."

"And what about Tom?" Quinn added. "Where have they taken him?"

"I will take you to the Guardian," Finn answered. "Your injured friend has already been taken to him. The Guardian will want to speak with you."

With Fergus and Wulfric trotting at their heels, Elanor, Quinn and Sebastian followed Finn along the foreshore. The shore was steep and rocky and waves crashed around them making the stone slippery with spray. The sky was ominous with thunderclouds and that shivery wind still blew, making Sebastian's arms prickle with goose bumps. Quickthorn's mane and tail were blown sideways. Quinn had to hold back her hair with both hands.

Finn led them up a steep pathway between stands of pine trees. The path led between two tall boulders, which guarded a heavy wooden gate, studded all over with sharks' teeth, and protected along the top and bottom by long sharp bones shaped like swords. Finn rapped on the gate three times, and it was unfastened and swung open by a fierce-looking warrior with a scarred face.

Sebastian came to an abrupt standstill. Once they stepped beyond the gate, it could be shut and fastened behind them, and he and his friends would be trapped. Finn seemed friendly enough, but he was scarcely human with his glinting scaly skin. Sebastian frowned and put his hand on his sword hilt.

Quinn saw his gesture. But they had no choice.

Tom, she mouthed.

She was right. Tom had been taken inside that gate. They had to go inside too. Slowly, reluctantly, Sebastian walked forward and the girls followed, Wulfric and Fergus at their heels.

"I need to shut the gate now," Finn said apologetically. "If the storm blows too high, the lagoon will rise and we don't want to risk any sea serpents getting in."

"Do they come ashore?" Sebastian asked.

"All the time," Finn answered. "They're slow and clumsy on shore, but we must keep a watch out for them and make sure we're always armed."

He swung the gate shut and fastened it securely, then led them down into the valley beyond. Surrounded on all sides by steep cliffs, the valley floor cradled a serene green lake. Willow trees grew around it, trailing their leafy branches in the water. Wicker boats were piled along the nearest shore, and a few floated on the lake, with people fishing from them. Quinn stared at them intently as they passed. They seemed to be larger versions of the tiny wicker boat that she had been found in as a baby . . .

A woman nearby was hoeing a vegetable patch. Her hoe was made with a large shell tied to a wooden handle. She was dressed in a crude dress made of some kind of thin skin, with a feathery fringe. Her hair hung in long, messy braids down her back. Her skin was darker than Quinn's, but not scaly like Finn's. She stopped to stare at them, shading her eyes with one hand, then turned and called out a name.

A child came running out of a small leafy hut which had been built from living willow trees. The trunks had been trained to grow into a dome shape, the fronds all cleverly woven together to make walls and a doorway. At the sight of Elanor and the unicorn, the child ran and hid behind his mother's leg, one thumb in his mouth. Elanor's eyes were just as wide in amazement at his curious home. She had never seen a house built in such a way before.

As she walked on, she saw many other willow houses built on the shores of the lake. "If you cut a branch from a willow tree and plant it in the ground, it will grow," Finn explained to her. "So whenever anyone needs a new house, we simply cut a pile of leafy branches, stick them in the ground, weave them in the shape we want and then leave them to grow and thicken."

"It must be cold in winter," Quinn said.

"Freezing," Finn admitted. "But we hang the inside of the houses with skins and furs, and every house has a fireplace. We have trouble getting enough fuel, though. Willow wood is very wet and takes a long time to dry out, and we never find enough seaweed or driftwood to burn."

"Do you all live here, in this valley?" Sebastian asked as he looked around.

"It's the only place that is safe," Finn said. "It was always a special place for us, with the lake and the willows, and so when the city was flooded, we fled here. We were saved by the willows; they're the most useful tree in the world."

Elanor saw evidence of this usefulness all around—baskets of all shapes and sizes, beehives and ropes, chairs and tables and stools, balls for children to kick around, fences and gates and even a bridge over a stream—all made of willow.

They reached the far end of the lake where a grove of ancient willow trees grew, their trunks thick and gnarled. Their crowns had been braided together to create a high domed roof, far above the ground. The last light of the day eased through the dome, creating a soft emerald glow. In the center was a great throne, shaped and woven from living wood. An old man sat hunched there, wearing a cloak made of gannet feathers. Around his neck was a ruff of orange-gold feathers, sweeping down to snowy white, the hem fringed in glossy black. In one hand was a tall staff of twisted willow wood, and he wore a talisman of a spiraling shell around his neck.

Despite the cloak, the old man's face looked pinched and cold. "I beg your pardon, my children," he said, his voice hoarse. "The witch wind bites through to the very marrow of my bones. It is worse than the storms of winter."

"Guardian, these are the sailors whose boat was shipwrecked by the sea serpents," Finn said. "They travel with many strange beasts."

"So I see," the old man replied, his blue eyes resting

upon the unicorn.

He had a gentle wrinkled face with a sunken mouth, his long white hair and beard hanging in the same matted elflocks as Finn's. When he smiled, Elanor saw he had very few teeth left. His fingers were crooked with age.

"Where's Tom?" Quinn asked.

"We have laid him out in the weeping room and tried to make him as comfortable as possible. We've given him willow bark tea which will help ease the pain and fever a little. You may watch over his last hours if you wish."

"His last hours?"

"The weeping room?"

"He's not going to die, is he?"

All three children burst into horrified words.

The Guardian gazed at them sadly.

"There is no cure for sea serpent's venom. I'm sorry, my children, to tell you such news. The venom will fester in his body and take him fast. Your friend will be gone by morning."

11

THE
GUARDIAN'S TALE

THE
GUARDIAN'S TALE

Elanor and her friends hurried through cavern-ous halls and galleries woven from living green willow. With the sun slanting low from the west, the willow leaves were lit to the most vivid emerald on one side, and yet were shadowed and gloomy on the other. They moved fluidly in the wind so that the walls and ceilings swayed and rustled and swished in the strangest way possible. Birds darted here and there above their heads and the air was full of their song.

Finn led them to a small willow chamber by the lake. Tom was laid out on a low bier made of woven branches. Thick white candles were set on tall wooden candleholders at the four corners of the bier. They flickered and smoked in the incessant wind, which kept the leaves fluttering.

A tall, angular-faced woman was sitting on a high-backed chair at the end of the bier. She wore a robe of white feathers and a circlet of pearls and turquoise on her head. She stood as they entered through the hanging willow fronds.

"Have you come to bid your friend farewell?" she asked sadly.

"No! There must be something we can do!" Quinn burst out, throwing herself down on her knees beside Tom. He was deathly white, his skin sheened with sweat. His foot and leg were swollen and discolored, the puncture wound oozing.

"Once, perhaps," the woman said. "But the wishing well is lost. The witch stole it from us. We have failed in every endeavor to win it back from her."

Elanor stared at Tom with wide shocked eyes. Quickthorn stepped close and bent his horned head to sniff at Tom's foot. Elanor caught the unicorn's halter in her hand, drawing his head away. Fergus whined and nosed Tom's limp hand and Wulfric whimpered, his front paws resting on the bier. Tom did not rouse.

"I don't understand," Sebastian said. "The witch? If there's a wishing well nearby, we need it!"

"Once, the magic of the wishing well may have helped you," the woman said. "But now all magic here is twisted awry. There is nothing we can do. I'm afraid you must say good-bye to your friend."

Quinn, Elanor and Sebastian could not speak. It seemed so wrong that their quest should end this way. As they stared down at Tom, so white and still, the woman turned her head and said to Finn, "Go and change out of your suit, my boy, you'll catch your death in this cold wind."

Finn nodded and slipped away into the gloom under the willow trees.

"I am Lady Nerissa," the woman said. "The kingdom that lies under the waves was my father's. This small valley is all that is left of what was once a proud city."

"I . . . I'm sorry," Elanor said. "But, please . . . what about Tom? We have to save him!"

Lady Nerissa's face was full of pity, but she said

nothing to reassure them.

"We cannot let him die," Quinn cried. "He mustn't!"

"Where is the wishing well?" Elanor asked. "What do we need to do to fix it?"

Lady Nerissa looked at her in surprise. "You cannot fix it. It's the witch's cursing well now, and she uses it to conjure all kinds of dark magic. She cannot be defeated. Believe me, we have tried and tried again. The very idea is impossible."

"I have come to realize that virtually nothing is impossible," Elanor said in a firm voice.

There was a moment of long silence. Nerissa looked taken aback. Then Sebastian laughed. He reached over and hugged Elanor close to his side. "Ela, you are right! Nothing's impossible! Tell us, what is this well and where can we find it?"

Nerissa looked distressed. "Indeed, I do not think you understand. The witch I speak of? She is a black witch of extraordinary power. She cannot be defeated."

"If the only way to save Tom is to defeat her, then that's what we must do," Sebastian said. "We have a few tricks of our own up our sleeve, I can promise you."

At that point Beltaine poked her head out of the top of Sebastian's jacket, blinking around sleepily. Everyone was surprised into smiles. It eased the tension and made them all feel a little more hopeful.

"We need to know everything about this witch," Quinn said.

"That is a tale for the Guardian to tell," Lady Nerissa said.

"While he tells it, I'll make a poultice for Tom's foot," Quinn said. "Please, I need honey and sea salt and crushed cypress leaves."

Nerissa quirked an eyebrow. "Well, I think I can manage that."

It was gloomy and quiet under the willow trees. The wind in the branches sounded like the susurration of the sea.

The Guardian sat on his throne, huddled in his tricolored cloak of feathers. Bowls of food had been brought—fish and damp seaweed and thin cockle soup. Sebastian grandly doled out food from their store—a leg of ham was fallen upon with such a chorus of delight that he grinned in happy surprise.

"We have not seen ham in many years," Lady Nerissa explained. "Indeed, I do not think Finn has ever tasted it."

Finn had come sidling out of the twilight, dressed now in rough and crudely made clothes. "But you were all scaly before," Elanor said. "I thought that was your skin."

Finn smiled. "Ha, no! We wear suits made of serpent skin when we go out into the water. It keeps us warm and stops our skin from shriveling."

Elanor stared at him. "Really? Are sea serpent skins easy to come by?"

"We hunt for them," Finn said with a shrug. "We've learned how to sew them into suits. We cannot make cloth here, you understand. The soil is so poor, and given over entirely to growing food."

"But how have your lives come to this?" Quinn exclaimed.

"It began a long time ago, long before any of you were born," the Guardian said. "I was a young man, then. Our kingdom was small, but rich and proud. Brightwell Island was the first port of call for anyone sailing east to west, or west to east. People came on a pilgrimage to our wishing well, famous across the seven seas. Anyone who had a deeply held desire could make a wish and feel it might come true. People came miles to wish for health or wealth or wisdom. I was the Well Guardian." He paused, his face furrowed with sorrow.

"Go on," Elanor said softly.

"One day, a small boat washed up on our shores. Inside was a beautiful woman with two little girls. The boat had no sail, no oars. She told us that she and her daughters were the sole survivors of a shipwreck and had been floating on the waves for days. We were sorry for her. We welcomed her and found her a place to stay . . ."

"If we had known the truth about her, we would have cast her off again," Lady Nerissa cried.

"What happened?" Sebastian asked. "Who was she? What did she do?"

"I have come to think it was no accident of wind and tide that brought her here," the Guardian went on. "I believe she used her witch powers to end up on our shores quite deliberately. She wanted our well."

"She wanted to make a wish?" Elanor asked.

"She wanted to cast a curse," he answered. "A curse on us and on others."

As he told the story, Quinn felt as if she could see the scene in her mind's eye. The beautiful woman with the huge black eyes so full of sorrow, clutching her little girls, begging for help . . . Her name was Githa, the Guardian said. The Lord of Brightwell Island was moved by her sorry plight. He gave her rooms in the castle and invited her to eat at his table.

"Githa had her eye on him," Lady Nerissa said, her voice full of anger. "I remember. She smiled and fluttered her eyelashes, but my father was still in love with my mother. They arranged for her to have a little cottage near the woods, away from the castle, but that wasn't enough for her."

"Strange, dark things began to happen," the Guardian said. "People who spoke out against her fell ill, or had accidents, or their businesses began to fail. Then Lady Nerissa's mother fell ill and her father seemed as if he walked everywhere in a dream."

Elanor drew in her breath sharply. It sounded just like what had happened with her own parents! "Then what happened?" she asked breathlessly.

"My mother died . . ." Lady Nerissa took up the tale, "and Githa was always at the castle, saying she had come to help. I grew to hate the sight of her. She was all sweet and soft with my father, but she was cruel to everyone else. She behaved as though she were a queen, and we were simply peasants under her boot. My father saw through her, though. He told her he would never marry her. And she told him he'd be sorry."

Lady Nerissa's eyes were bright with tears. Finn went and leaned against her and she hugged him close.

"I had been troubled by Githa for some time," the Guardian said. "Whenever a ship came in to harbor, I would go down and talk to the sailors, asking for news about ships that had gone down. No one knew of any lost ship." He leaned forward, his knuckles white on his staff. "Then, one day, I discovered the terrible truth about Githa and her daughters. But by then it was too late."

12

GITHA'S CURSE

Quinn gripped the oak medallion so tightly it cut into her hand. She knew, beyond a shadow of a doubt, that what she was about to hear would cast light on many a dark mystery.

"A sailor told me that King Gwydion of Storm-ness had died in most mysterious circumstances," the Guardian said. "He left behind two little boys, the eldest only seven. Prince Conway had been crowned king, but his uncle Ivor had been named Regent, to rule on his behalf till the boy was grown."

Quinn exchanged a startled glance with Elanor and Sebastian. It seemed that all the roads were leading to King Ivor.

"There were rumors that Prince Ivor had murdered his own brother. Many people feared for the lives of the young king and his brother." The Guardian gripped the head of his stick tightly, his jaw working in distress.

"However, the sailor told me that he had heard gossip that the palace witch had been set adrift in a boat as punishment for the crime. Her two little girls were set adrift with her. It was said that they were Prince Ivor's daughters, and that is why he did not have her killed for her crime."

"So this witch Githa had killed the king?" Quinn asked. "But why would she do that?"

"Perhaps she wanted to be queen," Lady Nerissa said. "Perhaps she tried to convince Prince Ivor to seize the throne after his brother died, but he refused. Perhaps the king had warned Prince Ivor against her."

"So Prince Ivor puts her and his two little daughters—his own daughters—in a boat, and sets them adrift?!" Elanor was white with horror.

"He suspected Githa of murdering his *brother*," Sebastian reminded her.

"He might even have had real proof of it," Finn suggested.

"Maybe so, but those two little girls were his daughters!"

"Maybe he did not believe this to be true," the Guardian said. "We cannot know what was in his mind. All we do know is that Githa and her daughters washed up here."

"We should have guessed that she had been exiled when we found her in a boat without sails or oars," Lady Nerissa said bitterly.

"I went hurrying to tell the lord, but he refused to believe me," the Guardian said.

"See, Githa had cast a spell on him!" Lady Nerissa cried. "He was a changed man."

Like Elanor's father, Quinn thought and glanced at her friend. Elanor looked white and miserable. She felt Quinn's glance and gave her a piteous look in return, but neither spoke.

"So I confronted Githa," the Guardian went on. "It was midwinter and the night of the dark moon, the most powerful time possible for working evil magic. I should have known. I should have guessed." He shook his snowy head.

"She cast a curse on you all?" Quinn guessed.

He nodded. "I tried to stop her. We fought for what seemed like hours. She was stronger than me, though, and she had her daughters to help her, whose powers were also growing. Githa has the ability to make small creatures great. With her magic, the adders and toads and newts that lived in the stone by the well became giants. It was all I could do to stay alive. Then—" The Guardian was unable to speak, his voice overcome with emotion.

"What happened?"

"She gave sight to the well . . ."

"She gave sight?" Quinn repeated. "What do you mean?"

"So that she could see and control all the oceans . . . she gave one of her eyes to the well."

"What?" Elanor clapped both hands to her mouth.

"You're joking!" Sebastian cried.

Quinn could not comprehend such an act.

"With this act, Githa gained power over the well.

She could command all those hideous giant creatures and she could order the seas to rise up and swallow Brightwell Island. And this is what she did. I saw it happen. The city was drowned, along with the castle and my lord. Only a few managed to survive."

There was a long silence before Lady Nerissa continued the horrid tale.

"The serpents slithered down to the sea and took over the drowned city. We built houses under the willow trees, and did what we could to survive."

"Githa stayed at the well," the Guardian said sadly. "It is a cursing well now. The water is poisoned. Evil airs rise from it and flow across the islands, making us all sick. As fast as we kill the serpents, she conjures more, and other dreadful creatures too. Scorpions and toads and eels, all at her command."

"We have tried to fight her, but she is too powerful. Now we do all we can to keep away from her," Lady Nerissa said.

"Githa has some kind of greater plan that we do not understand," the Guardian said. "She sent her daughters away some time ago. First she ordered the sea serpents to bring up the treasure chests from the drowned castle and she hung her daughters in pearls and rubies. Then she brought a merchant ship here with an enchanted wind."

"It was laden with silks and velvets," said Lady Nerissa. "She dressed her daughters as fine as princesses, boarded them on the ship and the sea serpents towed them away."

"We don't know where they went, but you can be sure they are out there somewhere now, spreading evil," the Guardian said.

Quinn looked at Elanor and Sebastian, a sudden idea sparking in her brain. "Could it have been Lady Mortlake, do you think?"

"Yes!" Elanor's eyes blazed with new understanding. "And Mistress Mauldred? Could it be?"

"They're sisters?" Sebastian cried.

"Working together all this time!" Elanor shook her head with anger.

"But why?" Sebastian demanded.

"To bring down the throne." Elanor was sure of it. "To seize it for themselves. If they really were King

Ivor's daughters, they must feel that the throne is rightfully theirs."

"How long ago was this?" Quinn asked.

"It was before Finn was born," Lady Nerissa said. "About fourteen years ago."

"Mistress Mauldred came to Wolfhaven Castle just before I was born," Elanor said. "I'll be thirteen soon."

"And that awful Cedric boy is thirteen too, so Lord and Lady Mortlake could have been married about fourteen years ago," Sebastian said.

The Guardian was looking at them in puzzlement, so Quinn turned to him and said, "We think we know where Githa's daughters ended up. And, if we're right, they're working together in a conspiracy to overthrow King Ivor and take over Stormness."

He nodded in sudden comprehension. "So Ivor is King of Stormness now, is he? What happened to the boy who was crowned king? Conway?"

"He died. And his brother Derwyn, too," Elanor said. "Some people think King Ivor killed them both."

"I would hazard a guess that it was Githa," the Guardian said. "And I can tell you how . . . There was a great storm one night about thirteen years ago. A ship was swept up on the rocks of Adderwell Island."

"That is what we call the island now," Finn explained in an undertone. "It is Brightwell no more."

"Everyone on board the ship was lost, except for one small baby, found in a cradle on the waves."

Quinn had only been half listening, her brain busy with thoughts of the evil sisters, Lady Mortlake and Mistress Mauldred, but this caught her attention. "Wait. What?"

"Just as my men found the baby, they heard Githa coming," Lady Nerissa said. "They hid and watched as she frantically searched through all the wreckage."

"What was she looking for?" Elanor asked.

Quinn listened eagerly for the answer. "Githa looked at the face of every body, washed up along the shore. She was very pleased when she found one particular man, and wrested a ring from his finger. She then found a chest and smashed it open."

"Inside were a crown, a scepter and a sword," Finn interjected eagerly.

Lady Nerissa nodded. "We think the dead man

must have been some kind of king."

"It was King Conway!" Elanor cried. "He was lost in a shipwreck thirteen years ago. Everyone thought it was a tragic accident, but it was Githa! Again!"

"But," Quinn began timidly, "what about the baby you found?" She almost didn't recognize her own voice.

Elanor's eyes went wide. She and Sebastian stared at Quinn in sudden comprehension.

"We guessed the baby was the one Githa was searching so desperately for," the Guardian said. "The men put the smashed cradle on the shore, so that Githa would think the baby had fallen out and drowned."

"We didn't know what to do. If we kept the baby and Githa found out, her vengeance would be terrible."

"She sees many things in that well of hers," the Guardian said. "We dared not risk it. We put the baby in a coracle, all wrapped up in her lacy shawl, and in the dark of the night, we put her out to sea. I summoned up the last of my powers and I cast a spell of concealment over her, and then I bespelled the little boat to take her safely to the east."

"Is a . . . coracle like those wicker boats your warriors were rowing today?" Quinn asked.

Lady Nerissa nodded.

"Did you put anything else in with the baby?" Quinn's voice was vibrating with intensity.

"Only one other thing," the Guardian said. "A silver rattle we'd found with her in the cradle."

Quinn gasped. She grabbed her bag and rummaged around inside. "Like this one?" she asked, holding up the silver rattle she had been given by old Willard.

"Yes!" The Guardian stared at her in utter surprise. "That's the rattle!"

"Then I was that baby," Quinn said.

13

SKULL OR CAULDRON

"That means you are the true queen!" Sebastian said, his excited voice cutting through the hubbub of exclamations and questions. "Don't you see? If the dead man was King Conway and you are his daughter . . . that means you should be queen."

"No," Quinn said, feeling strange and light-headed. "That can't be true. None of this can be true."

"It is!"

"No. It can't be. I'm just an ordinary girl. I must be the child of some other person on that ship. We've got it wrong."

"The cradle we found you in was not the cradle of an ordinary child," Lady Nerissa put in. "It was carved with some kind of shield."

Numbly, Quinn showed her the shield on the silver rattle.

"Yes, that's it. A dove carrying a heart," Lady Nerissa said.

Quinn felt a weird sort of slippage, as if she had been in this moment before, and heard those words spoken before.

"I hope it's true, because then we'd be cousins!" Elanor hugged Quinn.

Quinn did not hug her back. She said, in an odd, strained voice, "I cannot think about all that now. It's too awful and strange to be true. I'll think about it later. Right now, we have to think about Tom."

Lady Nerissa rose. "I shall take him more willow bark tea."

The children followed her back to the weeping room, where Tom lay silent and still. Fergus raised his head from where he lay beside his master and whined.

"The venom is working its way through his system," the Guardian said from behind them as Lady Nerissa trickled the steaming tea between Tom's lips.

It ran down his cheeks to pool by his ears. "He can no longer swallow the tea. Leave him be, my lady."

Quinn jumped up. "We have to figure out what to do! We have to beat that witch and turn that cursing well back into a wishing well. But how? There has to be something we can do!" She could scarcely take a breath, tears streaming down her face.

The Guardian's face was sad. "I'm sorry, my child. There is nothing that can save your friend."

"We must try!"

"I think we should leave you in peace with your friend," Lady Nerissa said. "Come, Finn."

"Call me if you need anything," Finn said, then with a sympathetic backward glance, he helped the Guardian hobble away, his mother sweeping behind.

Quinn's hand went to the bag of tell-stones at her belt. "I'll do a casting. The tell-stones will tell me what I must do!"

She dropped to her knees, feverishly clearing a space on the ground with one hand and shaking the bag with the other. Elanor and Sebastian dropped down beside her. It was very strange to have only three of them in the circle, and not all four. No one could bear to look at Tom, so pale and still on his bier.

One by one, Quinn pulled out tell-stones from the bag and laid them in a circle.

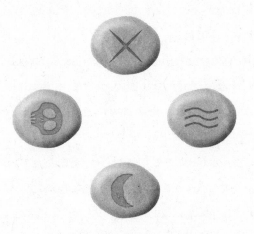

"Crossroads, a place of dilemma, a decision to be made," Elanor said. "Well, yes."

"Waves. That means change, doesn't it?" Sebastian said hopefully.

"Waves mean ebb and flow," Quinn said. "Waves bring things to you and take them away."

"That doesn't sound very hopeful," Elanor said.

"A Crescent Moon," Sebastian said. "What does

that mean?"

"It's a waning moon," Quinn said. "That is a time to work banishing magic, to reverse a spell or to drive something away."

"I'd definitely like to drive that witch away," Sebastian said hotly.

Quinn's hand stilled. "Yes," she said slowly. "There's an idea. I wonder what the moon is tonight? It was a full moon only a few days ago. It must be in its waning phase now."

She pulled out the last tell-stone, but in her haste her fingers were clumsy and she dropped it. The stone spun and landed sideways.

"It's the Skull," Elanor said. "That means death."

"Unless it is upside down," Quinn said. "Then it is not Skull, but Cauldron, and that means life."

"But it's neither up nor down," Sebastian said. "Look, it's halfway between the two."

"I think it means Tom is halfway between life and death," Quinn said, after a long pause. "He could go either way."

Elanor began sobbing.

"No, it's good news," Quinn said. "Everyone keeps telling us there's no hope, that Tom must die, but the tell-stones say differently. They say there is hope."

They all looked towards the bier where Tom lay. Quickthorn still stood beside him, his head bent down to his foot. Then he turned and gazed at them with intense dark eyes. He whinnied and pawed his hoof emphatically, and then bent his head to Tom's foot again.

Realization smote Quinn so hard she gasped. The answer had been with them all along.

"I am an idiot!" she cried.

"What do you mean?" Elanor looked at her in amazed distress, but Quinn did not listen. She threw all their packs apart, until she found a water bottle. She gave a cry of fierce satisfaction. It was full of fresh rainwater from the storm the night before.

"What do unicorns do with their horns?" she said over her shoulder as she raced towards Quickthorn.

"They heal," Elanor said softly. "You're right. We are fools."

"Quickthorn's horn could heal Tom?" Sebastian

asked. "If only we'd thought of it before. Do you think it's too late?"

"I hope not." Quinn held the water bottle out to the unicorn and he dipped his gleaming black horn in. As soon as the horn had been withdrawn, Quinn was bending over Tom. She poured some on the oozing wound in his black and swollen foot, then dripped some into his mouth. At first it just ran out of the corners of his lips, then Tom weakly swallowed.

"It's working!" Sebastian punched one fist into his other palm.

The three friends hung above Tom, dribbling more water into his mouth and bathing his foot until all the water was gone. It seemed to Quinn's anxious eyes that his color was a little better, and that his foot seemed less swollen.

"I think one of us should stay here and keep bathing it in enchanted water," she said to her friends. "I'm sure it'll help."

"While the rest of us go and tackle that witch!" Sebastian got to his feet, reaching for his sword.

"Yes." Quinn was finding another two water bottles

and holding them up for Quickthorn to dip his horn into. "Because I'm willing to bet that Quickthorn's horn will fix that cursed well too!"

14

VENGEANCE DELAYED

"The waning moon is just rising," Quinn said. "We shall need to be quick. Now is the best time for banishing magic."

She gazed out at the waters of the lagoon. It was twilight, and the waters were still and silvery blue. To the west, the sky was streaked with red, like smears left by bloody fingers. The peaks of the island stood black against the orange of a half-moon rising slowly in the east.

"Best not chat," Sebastian muttered. "Sound carries over the water."

The two of them were crouched in one of the little wicker basket boats, rowing swiftly across the lagoon.

The coracle felt incredibly small and flimsy, but it skimmed lightly across the water. Sebastian had his sword drawn, ready for any sea serpents who might try to stop them.

"Look!" Quinn pointed.

A white wake of water was arrowing for them. Sebastian braced himself as a triangular head lifted itself from the water, lidless eyes fixed on the coracle. As the head began to writhe higher and higher, there was suddenly a great *whoosh!* Rex dropped out of the sky, seized the sea serpent's head and dragged it out of the water with a glittering spray of water like ice shards. As the two beasts fought in the sky above them, Quinn's oars sent the coracle skimming away to the dark island brooding on the opposite side of the lagoon.

Adderwell Island. Quinn did not like the sound of that at all.

"No valor, no victory," Sebastian muttered under his breath. His hands were clenched tight on his sword hilt.

The coracle bumped into the rocks. Quinn and Sebastian scrambled to shore, then dragged the little wicker boat out of the water and stowed it behind a large boulder. Behind them there was an almighty splash, and then a high shriek of triumph from the griffin.

There was just enough light to see a path snaking up the steep hill. Quinn and Sebastian climbed it as fast as they could, using both hands and feet. Tiny bats flittered above the mountain peak, their wings sharp against the dusk sky. Somewhere an owl hooted, melancholy and mysterious, and then came a distant grumble of thunder.

The path seemed to go on forever. It was damp and slippery, and Quinn's feet kept sliding away from under her. Mist hung around the rocks, chilly and clammy. A fragment of a dream came to her, like a bruise on her spirit. Quinn remembered the vision of the shipwreck, and the baby in the cradle. That had been her! She had seen her own parents' death, and her rescue by the Guardian.

She was the true queen. Quinn could barely believe it.

What would it mean for her life, her future? Would her great-uncle try and kill her too, when he learned of her existence? Were they already after her? Quinn shivered violently.

"Are you cold?" Sebastian whispered. "Do you want my jacket?"

Quinn clutched her shawl tighter to her, shaking her head. "Just nerves," she whispered back.

It *was* cold, however, the chill deepening with every labored step. The air smelled like a newly turned grave. Quinn's fingers were stiff claws, her bare feet leaden weights. She slipped and fell, but struggled up again. Behind her, Sebastian muttered under his breath.

A giant toad leapt down from the rock above. It was the size of a cart horse, its slimy skin stippled with warts. Quinn only just managed to scramble away from its broad, flat feet, before it hopped again. Its gargantuan shape blotted out the moon.

As Quinn and Sebastian struggled upward, more giant toads jumped over them, their enormous webbed feet making a wet, thwacking sound as they hit the stone. Then Quinn heard a slither. A gigantic leech came sliding and sucking down the path, flat head held high as if scenting for blood. The two friends pressed themselves against the cliff face, barely daring to breathe. The leech flowed straight past them, searching—Quinn hoped—for bigger prey.

She kept on climbing, her breath sharp in her throat. At last she managed to crawl over the edge of the cliff. A small dell lay below them, like the hollow in the palm of a hand. Rocks stuck up all around, dark and menacing against the streaked sky.

Quinn and Sebastian clambered to the top of a boulder and peered over the edge. In the middle of the hollow was a low well, its top covered by a huge stone. Quinn observed it with despair. They would never be able to get the well uncovered without alerting the witch, so she couldn't simply pour the enchanted water into the well now and end all the evil.

Nearby was a stone cottage with a mossy roof, its garden a tangle of brambles and weeds. Foul-smelling smoke curled from its twisted chimney. Sebastian nudged Quinn, then lay his finger along his lips. He jerked his head towards the cottage and motioned for her to follow. Together, they crept silently and swiftly to the squat building. Quinn lay down her staff by her feet and levered herself up to the small window. Sebastian crouched by her, his sword lying unsheathed across his knees, and kept a breathless lookout.

". . . don't see what is so *difficult*," a voice hissed from within the cottage. "Four mewling urchins, yet none of you have stopped them!"

Quinn peered in the window to see a woman leaning over an obsidian ball on a battered table. Her slinking, glittering dress was made from snakeskin and her hair flowed like black serpents down her back, almost to her knees. It hung in great hanks over her face, which was obscured from Quinn's eyes. "Need I remind you what is at stake? Time is running out."

"You've not done any better, Mother!" The voice came from the ball, distorted by the magic. "I sent them to you to take care of. What have *you* managed?"

Sebastian tugged at Quinn's ragged hem. "*Mistress Mauldred,*" he mouthed at her when she looked down. Quinn nodded imperceptibly. She remembered the shrill voice of Elanor's governess very well.

"The foundling girl has gained her powers," Mistress Mauldred continued. "The little witch nearly killed Ailith during the Harvest fire."

"Your sister is even more of a disappointment than *you* are," Githa snarled. "She insists on flitting around after that lumbering jackanapes of a husband. Our ends would have been met long ago if he didn't pursue his petty grudges. What use have I for Wolfhaven?"

"Do not speak ill of my husband, Mother!" A new voice joined the conversation. Quinn could hardly recognize Lady Mortlake's usually syrupy-sweet tones with the fury that came from the obsidian ball. "He has done admirably. And he will make a fine king. Once our armies are prepared—"

"*Your* armies?! Pah! *I* was the one who showed you how to raise the dead, girl. Don't forget to whom you owe *everything*!" Githa slammed her fist against the table. "The plan was simple! You and that fool husband were to go to Stormholt long ago, ready to take that throne. I have spent thirty years planning and sacrificing, I will wait no longer! Your *father*"— Githa spat out the word "father" as though it were a toad sitting upon her tongue—"still sits on that throne."

"Have patience, Mother," Mistress Mauldred said. "You will have vengeance. Let us complete our plans here—"

"Plans, ha!" Githa hissed. "All I hear from you is 'plans.' Fourteen years, and only 'plans.' The time has come for *action*." She leaned closer to the ball. "I sent you to Stormness dressed as *princesses*, as princesses you rightfully are! It could not have been simpler. Mortlake needed a wife. I arranged it so Wolfgang would need one too, yet *you*, Niniane, could not even complete that simple task *in eight years*."

Quinn stifled a gasp. They had suspected that Mistress Mauldred was behind the death of Elanor's mother, but to hear it so coldly stated was a shock nevertheless.

"You were ladies of society, ready for court. You were poised to destroy your faithless father," Githa was saying. "And then what? *Children. Husband. Greed. Delays!*"

"My children are not 'delays,' Mother," Lady Mortlake retorted coldly. "My husband has a plan that will work. We have spoken of this many times before! It is too dangerous to attack Stormholt directly. We had to work in shadows and secrecy. You agreed to wait, to let him set the pace of our vengeance! We must trust in him and we will be victorious."

"*Trust?!*" Githa shrieked. "You dare speak to me of *trust?* After all that has happened, after all I have taught you?" She jerked her hand and Quinn flinched at the magical blow she felt lash out in all directions. She stumbled down next to Sebastian, clutching at her skull. The two witches in the obsidian ball cried out in pain.

"Mother, stop!" Mistress Mauldred screamed.

"How did *love* and *trust* work out for you, Niniane?" Githa taunted over her daughters' screams. "How long did you wait for that cowardly fool Wolfgang to *reject* you?" She waved her hand and the pain in Quinn's head abruptly ceased. "Enough! I tire of delays, I tire of your excuses. Those four miserable infants are within a hair's breadth of destroying everything. This ends tonight. Ivor dies *tonight*. If nothing else, *I will have my revenge*."

And then, with another wave of her hand, she cut off her daughters' protests and strode out into the suddenly silent night.

15

THE
CURSED WELL

Sebastian and Quinn crept around the curve of the witch's cottage. In the murky moonlight, they could see her striding to the well, catching up a brimming basket that stood by the door.

"She'll never get that stone off the well," Sebastian muttered hopefully.

Githa uttered an incantation and the lid of the well flew off with a grinding of stone upon stone.

"Too much to hope for," Quinn whispered wryly. They crept closer, moving through the shadowy brush in the dell and taking care not to slip on the cold shingle below their feet.

The witch swayed, raised her arms high and began chanting a spell:

> "I INVOKE THEE, DARKEST OF GODS,
> I CALL ON THEE IN THIS DARK HOUR,
> AID ME IN MY DARK DEEDS,
> GIVE ME THE DARKEST OF POWER."

Githa twisted in the moonlight and Sebastian saw with a sickening wrench of his stomach that she had only one eye. The witch bent and picked up a great bunch of weeds from a basket at her feet, and threw them into the well:

> "WITH HEMLOCK AND RUE,
> I MAKE THIS WICKED BREW.
> REVENGE WILL HAVE ITS DAY
> I WILL MAKE HIM PAY.
> WITH BRIMSTONE AND GRAVE DIRT,
> I'LL MAKE HIM HURT.
> I'LL TAKE MY ENEMY AND SMITE, SMITE, SMITE,
> SCORN HIM, BREAK HIM, IN THE NIGHT."

Githa danced as she chanted, throwing ingredients into the well as she named them. Her hair swirled around her.

> "WITH ASHES OF BONE,
> I'LL SHAKE HIM FROM THE THRONE.
> NOTHING BUT SORROW AND GRIEF,
> FOR MY POOR HEART'S THIEF."

The witch was whipping herself into a frenzy of anger. Her crazed laughter rang out as she emptied a pitcher of ashes into the well. Mist began to rise from the waters, pouring over the lip of the well and wreathing around her bare feet.

> "MUD FROM A BLOODY BATTLEGROUND,
> HAIR FROM A KING WHO DROWNED . . ."

Quinn gasped and flinched. The sound was only slight, but the witch paused and looked around. Both Quinn and Sebastian pressed themselves low to the stony ground.

For a long moment, all was silent. Then the witch drew a long black knife out of the scabbard at her waist, and beckoned. Out of the shadows sidled a gigantic scorpion. It was far larger than the witch, but it crept towards her with its belly pressed close to the ground, its black and barbed tail hanging low. She gestured it closer and closer, then, with a swipe of the knife, slashed off its tail. It fell into the well with a hiss and a bubble. Smoke swirled up around her knees, as the injured scorpion scuttled away.

The witch beckoned again, and a sea serpent slithered into the hollow. From their vantage point, Sebastian and Quinn could easily see its black-patterned back as it writhed towards the well.

"WITH SCORPION'S TAIL
AND SEA SERPENT SCALE,
THE LAST PUMP OF SNAKE HEART'S BLOOD,
THE KING'S PULSE SHALL CEASE TO THUD.
ON HIS HEAD SHALL FALL MY BLIGHT,
ALL LIGHT SHALL FADE FROM HIS SIGHT."

Githa then raised her gleaming knife towards the sea serpent.

"She's going to kill the king! We have to stop her," Quinn hissed. "Sebastian, distract her! I'll get to the well and pour the unicorn water in."

She crept to the edge of the boulder and slipped down into the shadows. Sebastian huffed a great sigh, but was close behind her.

All was black and gray. The giant serpent was twisting and turning as the witch carved a scale from its pale upper belly. Quinn crept around the edge of the hollow, her pulse thundering so loud in her ears she was sure the witch would hear it.

"Distract her. Great," Sebastian muttered. With a deep breath, he stepped into the pale moonlight. "Hey!" he shouted, waving his sword. "Stop what you're doing!"

The witch whipped around, her black hair flying out around her body. For the first time, Quinn saw her face. Once, Githa would have been a beautiful woman, with high cheekbones and fine alabaster skin. But now her face was gaunt, her beauty ruined by the shadow where her left eye had once been.

Githa's astonishment gave way to mocking laughter. "Look, it's a boy who thinks he's a man. What do you do here, boy? You think you can stop *me*?" She let the sea serpent scale drop and sauntered towards him.

"Sure," Sebastian replied cockily. "Look at you, you're as skinny as a toothpick. And you only have one eye. I bet I could beat you with both eyes closed."

Githa hissed with impatience and rushed at him. Sebastian dived out of reach, rolled and came up with his sword swinging. It clanged against the witch's black dagger and broke in two.

"Argh!" Sebastian dropped his broken sword and backed away, both hands held high.

The witch darted at him again and Sebastian scrambled away. Githa stalked after him, dagger held at the ready. "Come here, boy," she taunted. "Come and prove that you're a man."

Quinn rushed to the abandoned well. Her fingers were shaking so much that she could scarcely draw the leather bottle of enchanted water from her belt or pull free the wooden stopper.

Githa whirled to face her. "I see you," she hissed. "I know you."

Quinn's hand stilled as though she was paralyzed. The words echoed in her mind . . . *I see you, I know you.*

Githa moved sinuously towards her, smiling. "But do you know yourself? I think not."

Tears burned Quinn's eyes.

"You are blood of the blood I have sworn to spill, leaf of the root I have sworn to dig out. I thought you were dead. Why aren't you dead?"

Quinn managed to speak. "I live because of the kindness of strangers."

The witch was angered. "Pah! *Kindness?* Stupidity!"

"Kindness shall always win over cruelty," Quinn said, though each syllable was like a stone she had to spit from her mouth. "Love shall always win over hate . . . in the end."

The witch rushed at her, hair swirling, her one eye blazing with madness. Quinn exerted all her strength and pulled the stopper from the bottle. She lifted it high, though it felt as heavy as lead, and poured a few drops into the well. Instantly, the mist began parting and rolling away. The half-moon looked down at her, like a pale face watching from a black hood.

"I banish your curse!" Quinn shouted, panting. "I banish your spell."

"No!" The witch struck at her, but Sebastian seized the sea serpent's scale from the ground and thrust it like a shield between them. The witch's knife hit the gleaming scale and instantly shattered into shards.

"No!" the witch screamed again, looking in horror at what was once her knife. "You fools! You think you can stand against me?"

Tears spilled over Quinn's eyelids and crept down her face. "You killed my parents. You tried to kill me. And now you attack my father's uncle."

"He should have made me queen," Githa spat. "The sacrifices I made for him! Yet he rejected me. Put me in a boat and sent me into exile. I swore revenge on him. All these years I have worked to see my revenge exacted. Two piddling children will not stop me."

"No?" Sebastian asked. "I think we have already."

The witch said to Quinn, "You think to turn my cursing well into a wishing well? It's not so easily done. I sacrificed my own eye to gain power over it. Whatever it is you have in that bottle of yours, do you think it can break such dark magic? I think not."

Quinn's shoulders sagged. It was stupid of her to think the witch's power would be so easily broken. She wiped her tears away with both hands.

"Don't listen to her." Sebastian's voice shook.

Quinn leaned above the well and poured a few more drops of the unicorn's enchanted water in. Her tears slipped down her face and fell in, too. The mist lifted like a veil, revealing the scene like an old engraving on silver. The one-eyed witch. The sea serpent lying in limp coils. The well, glimmering in its circle of stones.

"I wish . . ." Quinn paused, trembling.

"You could be queen," Githa crooned. "Just one wish, and it could happen."

Quinn shook her head. "No. I . . . no."

"Don't you wonder if your parents ever loved you? I know you have. I see the wound in your soul. All you have to do is look. Do it. Find out who you truly are, where you truly belong."

"No . . ."

"All you need is one wish," Githa whispered. "One wish only."

"Leave her alone," Sebastian cried.

The witch turned her eye upon him. "I see your wounded heart, too. Your longing. Quick! Here's your chance. Make your wish. Anything you want could be yours. You could be the greatest warrior in the world! Men would fall to their knees before you. The girl you love would love you back." Her stained teeth flashed in a blazing smile of triumph. "Your father would be *so* proud of you."

"Stop it!" Sebastian shouted.

"Just make the wish, boy. It could all be yours. *She* could be yours. It lies within your grasp." Githa's voice lowered to a tantalizing purr.

Sebastian looked imploringly at Quinn, desperate to silence the witch. "Do it! Make the wish!"

"I don't know what to wish for!" she screamed.

"Yes, you do!" Sebastian shouted back.

Quinn's mind was buzzing with wishes like a wintering box for bees. Deep in her mind, she heard Sylvan speak: *Stand strong like an oak in a storm, little maid. You have one wish only. Use it wisely.*

Quinn looked up at the moon. A waning moon, used for banishing and releasing. Calm fell upon her.

"I wish that I could turn back the tide of time and undo all the harm that this witch has caused. I wish that I could raise the drowned city from the deep and give breath to all those that are among us no more. I wish that murder could be undone and death could be reversed. But some things are, and should be, impossible. All I can do is make sure you do no more harm."

Quinn took a deep breath and leaned over the well, which was as still as a silver mirror. Her tears fell down and disturbed its serene surface. She spoke to her rippling reflection, all pale face and dark hair.

"I want to banish death and despair from this place. I want to banish malice and venom and curses. So this is what I wish. Let life triumph tonight, and love, and kindness, and mercy. Let those who travel in the shadow lands return unscathed. Let those who have been kind be rewarded and let those who are cruel be punished."

Like drops of ice, her tears fell into the dark well.

Drip. Drip.

The well water rippled like quicksilver, then all was still.

16

»——→WISHES←——«

For a long moment, there was nothing but silence. Then Githa covered her face with her hands. "No!" she screamed. "So close! So close to triumph!"

A dry rustling rose from the darkness. The giant serpent was moving, coiling, rising. Its sinuous shape twisted like a shadow against the silver moon. Then it struck and struck and struck again. The witch crumpled to the ground.

Then, most strangely, the sea serpent writhed close to Quinn and laid down its head at her feet, the great supple body winding around her in submission. Quinn bit her lip, then raised her hand up to the unblinking face.

"Quinn, no!" Sebastian gasped, lunging forward as though to stop her.

"Shhhh," she whispered, and with a deep breath, braced her hand on the great curving neck. The serpent was silky and cool under her fingers, not at all slimy like she had expected. Quinn poured the last drops of enchanted water on the wound in its chest. She watched in amazement as the gash slowly closed and healed. Then she bent and picked up the sea serpent scale from the ground. It was light but tough, glinting silvery in the moonlight.

"I think we've done it," she said shakily.

Sebastian released his breath and whooped in excitement. He picked her up and spun her around. "I think we have!"

"We need to go and see if Tom is awake," Quinn said. She could not look at the witch, lying in a heap of ragged snakeskin beside the well.

"Of course he's awake! Oh, Quinn, well done! I was so afraid you'd make the wrong wish."

"You could have wished yourself."

"I would have made the wrong wish for sure.

I'd have wished for roast pork, or a new sword, or something stupid."

"No, you wouldn't." Even as Quinn reassured him, she remembered the way Githa had tempted Sebastian with visions of power and glory and romance. She wondered what the witch had meant. What girl did Sebastian want to love him and why was his heart wounded? Was it Elanor? She had guessed that Lord Ashbyrne had sent his son to Wolfhaven in the hopes of a match one day between Sebastian and Elanor. She eyed him speculatively, but decided not to embarrass him by asking.

Sebastian grinned at her, unaware of where her thoughts had led her. "It wasn't my wish to make, anyway. It was your tears that worked the magic."

Quinn felt giddy with joy and relief. "Maybe you're right."

"Of course I'm right! Come on. Let's go. Don't forget the sea serpent scale."

Quinn hoisted it up and turned to go. But every step she took, the sea serpent writhed after her. She looked back. The sea serpent's great eye gazed at her imploringly. Quinn's heart beat rapidly as she met its gaze. "Very well, then. You can come, too."

They turned to go before Quinn halted suddenly as though she had walked into an invisible wall. "Wait!" she said, one hand pressed to Sebastian's rumpled doublet to hold him back.

Sebastian stared at her. "What?"

Quinn looked over her shoulder at the squat cottage, sitting alone in the dell. "Githa has lived there for years, wreaking her deadly spells. Should we search her cottage?"

"For what?" Sebastian asked. "Everything inside is probably as foul as she is."

"I don't know," Quinn said. "But I can't help but think we might find something that's useful." She stared blankly at the cottage, her mind a million miles away. Sebastian watched her for a minute.

"Your parents," he murmured. "You think she kept something of theirs?"

"I just don't know!" Quinn burst out. "Perhaps she did?" She looked at Sebastian pleadingly. He shrugged.

"It can't hurt to look," he said. "But what are you

going to do with your new friend here?" He motioned to the serpent that gazed at her with lidless adoration.

Quinn chewed her lip as she thought. "I'll go in," she eventually declared. "I'll have a better idea of what might be useful. And maybe something will spark a memory in me. You can stay outside with the serpent and keep watch."

Sebastian couldn't disguise his shudder at the thought of being left with the serpent. "Very well," he agreed begrudgingly. "Though I wish I still had my sword if I'm going to be around him."

"Oh, shush," Quinn chided, as she led the way back down to the cottage. "He's perfectly lovely."

"Lovely. Right." Sebastian dubiously eyed the huge snake slithering behind them. "Whatever you say."

Quinn eased open the door to Githa's cottage, gagging slightly at the rotten smell of decay that lingered inside. There was just one room, a cracked and sagging hearth dominating one wall. A rough pallet was crammed into one corner, but despite its makeshift frame, a velvet and fur cloak was thrown over it as a bedspread. When Quinn looked closer, she could just make out a crowned heart in the tarnished gold embroidery.

She'd seen that insignia before, on the royal pennants that flapped when King Ivor's messengers had come to Wolfhaven. Could this once have been the king's cloak?

She shook off her curiosity and bent her mind to the task at hand. There was a large chest at the foot of the bed, but it was filled with the foul paraphernalia of Githa's black magic. Quinn recoiled in disgust and the lid fell with a thump. Bunches of herbs hung from the rafters, but she was loath to touch them, let alone use them in any spell of her own. She left them where they were.

Quinn could hear Sebastian grumbling outside as she pushed the debris off a battered chest of drawers. The drawers were stuck, warped by the damp air and smoke, but she finally pulled one open with a groan of tortured wood. Spiders scuttled away as she peered inside. Her eye was caught by an iron box, bound and locked, no bigger than a loaf of bread. As she looked around for something to pry it open with, the back of her neck prickled with unease as if someone were watching her. She spun around in time to catch a flash of red glint from the obsidian ball.

Quinn gulped. Had she imagined the cruel face within the depths of the ball? Her flesh crept all over with tiny icy pinpricks. With a muttered oath, she seized the cloak from the bed and flung it over the obsidian ball. "Try spying on me through *that*," she whispered.

"Come on, Quinn, we need to go!" Sebastian

poked his head in the door. "Hey, what's that?" He was looking at the iron strongbox in her hands.

"I don't know. I can't get it open."

"Let's take it with us. Someone in Willowmere will be able to get it open."

Quinn and Sebastian rode across the lagoon perched on the neck of the rippling sea serpent, under the serene gaze of a high-sailing humpbacked moon. Quinn carried the serpent scale on her arm like a mother-of-pearl shield, while Sebastian clutched the iron strongbox.

"Now this is traveling in style!" she joked, as the serpent sped through the water.

"If only we could just ride him home," Sebastian laughed. She smiled at him.

"All that's left to do is wake the sleeping heroes," she said. "Can you believe it?"

"After everything that's happened tonight? It'll be the easiest thing we've ever done!" Sebastian grinned cockily at her.

Quinn had to smile and hope with all her heart that he was right.

The welcome sight of Elanor and Tom, leaping and laughing on Willowmere's moonlit shore, made it all seem possible.

17

LETTERS FROM THE PAST

"So what made you pick this up?" Tom asked Quinn. He had been examining the iron box carefully as his friends caught him and Elanor up on what had happened on Adderwell. They were sitting around a fire in the willow house that the Guardian had given to them as lodgings.

"Quinn?" Tom prompted.

Quinn shook her head. "I don't know. But it's like it called to me somehow."

"Here we go," Finn announced as he strode into the room. He waved a heavy hammer made of bone and stone. The four friends watched as he jammed a dagger against the box's padlock.

The hammer swung once, twice, and with a clang the old iron lock clattered to the ground. With a deep breath, Elanor eased open the lid. For a moment, it looked as though there was nothing inside. Sebastian huffed out his breath.

"Well, *that* was exciting," he said.

"No, wait!" cried Elanor. "Look here!" There was a slim parcel inside the box, cunningly wrapped in black velvet to disguise it among the felted box walls. Under the velvet, the parcel was wrapped again in waterproof snakeskin. And inside that, the parcel held four letters yellowed with age.

"Look!" Sebastian pointed to the first. "That's King Ivor's seal."

The first letter was written on heavy folded parchment and topped with a cracked ruby-red seal showing the crowned heart that Quinn had seen on the royal cloak in Githa's cottage. The creases of the parchment were well-worn and soft like old leather, as though someone had folded and refolded it over and over again. Elanor eased the letter gently open and began to read the bold script.

By order of His Highness, Prince Ivor
Lord Regent of the Ten Dominions and Stormholt

This hereby declares that Githa, lately Royal Lady Teller of King Gwydion, is banished from Stormholt Castle and the Ten Dominions of Stormness. She stands accused of highest treason, the murder of His Royal Majesty, King Gwydion. It is the Lord Regent's decree that she will not be put to trial, nor shall she face the executioner's sword. The lady is hereby stripped of her lands and title. She will be sent out of the kingdom along with her daughters, never to return on pain of death. She is to be granted no parley or commuted sentence. She is not permitted to contact the Lord Regent by any means.

This sentence shall be carried out forthwith, by royal order.

Signed,

Ivor

Domine Princeps Regent

The four friends stared at each other in shock. Finn ran his finger over the seal.

"So the Guardian was right," he mused. "Githa was banished by King Ivor for murdering the old king."

"But why didn't he have her executed?" Elanor asked. "It says here he's the one responsible for commuting her sentence to banishment."

Quinn lifted the second letter. It was written in a rushing, desperate scrawl on similar parchment to the first, but it was water stained. She read aloud:

My dear lord, my love, Ivor,

For all the love I bore you and bear you still, for our children, our girls, so young and innocent, I beseech you, my lord, have pity on a poor woman. Quell your rage at my actions, for I tell you truly, I have only ever acted out of love for you. You are the heart of my heart, the soul of my soul, and I wished to see you advanced to the position that should always have been yours. I bore your brother no ill will,

*but I could see, even if you could not, that he
stood in the way of your greatness. I could see
this because of my love for you. Your brother
was always a weak man. He would have seen
Stormness ruined. My love, can you not see
what my adoring eyes clearly see? You are
the one destined to bring our kingdom into a
glorious age! I implore you, bring me home.
Bring home our daughters. You shall be a great
ruler, and I will forever be by your side.*

Yours in eternity,

Githa

Quinn raised her eyes to Elanor's. "She killed the
old king *out of love?*" she whispered in horror.

Elanor shook her head. "It breaks my heart to hear
her beg so desperately," she said.

"Breaks your heart?" Tom asked incredulously.
"She was a murderess! And she sounds quite mad!"
He stared at the letter with revulsion.

"Now we know why he didn't have her executed,"

Finn observed. "He must have loved her but been horrified by her at the same time."

"And felt guilty," Sebastian added. "She says that she did it for him. He must have felt responsible for his brother's death." He looked at the other letters. "Do you think they have kept writing all these years? Is that what those other letters are?" He reached for the next letter in the pile. "She wrote this one, too."

Your Royal Highness,

I see now that the love you swore to me was naught but a sham. You have used me ill and now that your ends are met, you have no further use for me. My letters have all been returned to me, unopened. If you would trouble to read just one, you would know how your daughters suffer here in this wasteland, how I have suffered. But your cold heart cannot be touched. Well, I will beg no longer. I swear to you, you will pay for the hurt you have caused me.

Githa

"Love becomes bitterness," Tom whispered. "Bitterness and madness." He looked over at his friends. "Then this is how it all began. This is when she began plotting her revenge."

"And planned to drown our home," Finn added. "All because her letters weren't read?"

Quinn shook her head and took the letter from Sebastian. "It's not about the letters," she said. "She sees it as the biggest betrayal that King Ivor didn't stand by their love. And she can't understand that King Ivor saw her murderous actions in the same way." She glanced at Tom. "I think you're right. I think she was always just a little bit mad, and this tipped her over the edge."

"There's only one more letter left," said Elanor. "She must have destroyed all the others that he returned to her. It must have been too painful to keep them when he had rejected her so thoroughly." She picked it up with shaking fingers. It was hardly a letter at all, only a ragged scrap of parchment. "I'm almost afraid of what it will say."

She read the browned words aloud.

You have heard by now of what I have done to your accursed nephew and his spawn. I have dug out that root and twig of your blasted tree. And I am coming for all of you. You, Ivor, I will leave till last. You will see your beloved family turn to ashes before you. You will see all your heart's desires crumble and die. Your tree will bear no fruit of its own, for you have robbed my daughters of their birthright. I will restore their fortunes. I will raise them to the throne that they deserve. And I then will crush you under my heel as you rue the day you ever betrayed me.

The fire crackled and spat in the silence.

Quinn was trembling from head to toe. Sebastian wrapped his jacket around her. "My parents . . ." she whispered. "She's gloating about killing my parents and my uncle Derwyn."

Elanor dropped the letter and reached over to hug her friend tightly. "She had lost her mind completely by then, Quinn. I don't think she was even human. She was truly lost to evil."

Tom frowned. "But why would she write that?" he asked. "The king wasn't reading her letters."

The others watched as Quinn squinted at the letter, turning it this way and that in the firelight. Finally, she gingerly sniffed the paper.

"Ugh! It stinks of henbane."

"What does that mean?" Elanor asked.

"They call it the devil's eye," Quinn answered. "It means that she *did* get him to read this. Whether he wanted to or not." She looked at her friends. "There is a particularly dark spell Arwen once told me about. It lets you cast messages into the dreams of others. 'Written in blood, written in fire,' Arwen used to say. I think Githa burned this message straight into the king's mind. You can't ignore a message like that."

The FACE IN THE LAKE

The fire had sunk low. Quinn sat, her arms hugging her knees, staring across the shimmering lake. Finn had returned to his home. Her three friends lay sleeping, heads pillowed on their arms. The animals all slept too, snoring gently in the fresh sea air.

She was weary too, but unable to sleep. *What would happen now?* The witch sisters would not be pleased at the death of their mother. She was sure they had seen her through the obsidian ball before she had thought to cover it. Already Quinn could feel the wind rising, the sea beginning to swell.

The lake glimmered nearby. It caught the pale radiance of the moon, the dark vault of the starry sky, the warm sheen of the dying fire. Near the shore, by Quinn's foot, it eddied and spun, coalescing into the image of an old woman's face.

Quinn . . .

Quinn startled upright. "Arwen?"

Quinn, can you hear me?

She bent over the water, her heart skittering in her chest. "Yes . . . I'm here . . ."

You must hurry . . . the witches are in a rage . . . they are summoning such a storm! What have you done? What has happened?

"We defeated their mother," Quinn whispered. "She was a black witch who caused the deaths of the last three kings of Stormness. She tried to kill King Ivor tonight, but we foiled her."

Is she dead? Tell me, is she dead? Arwen's thread-thin whisper was urgent.

Quinn nodded. "The sea serpent killed her. We have all four beasts, now, Arwen! We have all four ingredients for the spell."

You must hurry! The witches thirst for revenge. They swear we shall all die in payment for their mother's death.

They had hoped to win the throne by stealth and secrecy. Now their only hope is to take Stormholt Castle by force. They plan to trick the king into thinking it is Lord Wolfgang who attacks . . . hurry . . . there is little time . . .

Arwen's pale face and silvery hair were dissolving into shaken patterns of light on the water.

"No!" Quinn cried. "Arwen, please, no! I need you."

I speak to you through a puddle on our prison floor. In the same puddle, I have seen my fate. My days are numbered. The thread of my life is caught on the blade. The only hope is to awaken the four heroes that sleep below the castle . . . but you must be quick . . . hurry . . . I beg you . . . hurry . . .

The Grand Teller's face dissolved into shadows.

"Arwen!" Quinn cried. "Please, come back! I have so much to tell you. Oh, please . . . Arwen."

Her voice was lost in the rising scream of the wind, clawed and fanged with magic. Quinn's hair whipped wildly. Then lightning stabbed straight through the water, shattering the last lingering reflections of the Grand Teller's face.

Quinn sat back on her heels, shaking with despair.